T0282799

furever
after

furever after

A MAGICAL CATS MYSTERY

SOFIE KELLY

BERKLEY PRIME CRIME
new york

BERKLEY PRIME CRIME
Published by Berkley
An imprint of Penguin Random House LLC
penguinrandomhouse.com

Copyright © 2024 by Penguin Random House LLC
Penguin Random House supports copyright. Copyright fuels creativity, encourages diverse
voices, promotes free speech, and creates a vibrant culture. Thank you for buying an
authorized edition of this book and for complying with copyright laws by not
reproducing, scanning, or distributing any part of it in any form without permission.
You are supporting writers and allowing Penguin Random House to continue to
publish books for every reader.

BERKLEY and the BERKLEY & B colophon are registered trademarks and
BERKLEY PRIME CRIME is a trademark of Penguin Random House LLC.

Library of Congress Cataloging-in-Publication Data

Names: Kelly, Sofie, 1958– author.
Title: Furever after / Sofie Kelly.
Description: New York: Berkley Prime Crime, 2024. |
Series: A Magical Cats Mystery
Identifiers: LCCN 2024000806 (print) | LCCN 2024000807 (ebook) |
ISBN 9780593548738 (hardcover) | ISBN 9780593548752 (ebook)
Subjects: LCSH: Cat owners—Fiction. | Librarians—Fiction. |
Cats—Fiction. | Murder—Investigation—Fiction. |
LCGFT: Cozy mysteries. | Novels.
Classification: LCC PR9199.4.K453 F87 2024 (print) |
LCC PR9199.4.K453 (ebook) | DDC 813/.6—dc23/eng/20240109
LC record available at https://lccn.loc.gov/2024000806
LC ebook record available at https://lccn.loc.gov/2024000807

Printed in the United States of America
1st Printing

This is a work of fiction. Names, characters, places, and incidents either are the product of
the author's imagination or are used fictitiously, and any resemblance to actual persons,
living or dead, business establishments, events, or locales is entirely coincidental.

For Lauren and Patrick, my own happy ending!

furever
after

chapter 1

It was déjà vu all over again.

The body was smack in the middle of my freshly scrubbed kitchen floor. Fred the Funky Chicken, minus his head. Earlier I'd found Ferdinand the Funky Frog, Fred's sibling by adoption, in the middle of the bedroom floor. He'd also been decapitated.

"Owen!" I said sharply.

Nothing.

"Owen, you little furball, I know you did this. Where are you?"

There was a muffled "meow" from the living room. I leaned around the doorway. The cat was sprawled on his back in the big wing chair, a neon yellow feather stuck to the top of his head. He rolled over onto his side and looked at me with the same goofy expression he always wore when he'd gotten into his catnip stash.

I crossed the room and sat down on the footstool. Owen lifted his head to look at me. His golden eyes didn't seem to be able to properly focus on my face. "Owen, you killed Fred," I said. "And then you killed Ferdy. This has got to stop."

He stretched and sat up slowly. Then he put a paw on my knee and tipped his head to one side as he tried to figure out how much trouble he was really in. The yellow feather was still stuck to the top of his head.

I held out my right hand. "Give me Fred's head," I said. The cat looked at me, eyes narrowed, seemingly trying to feign ignorance about what I was asking. "C'mon, Owen, give it to me."

He made a sound like a sigh then and spit what was left of Fred the Funky Chicken's head into my hand. It was a soggy lump of cotton with a stump of feather stuck on the end.

"You have a problem, Owen," I told the little gray-and-white tabby. "You have a monkey on your back." We'd had this conversation many times before. I looked down at the chewed-up chicken head. "Or maybe I should say you have a chicken on your back."

His response was to move closer and nuzzle my chin.

I plucked the feather from the top of his head and stroked his fur. Across the room I heard a soft "murp." Owen's brother,

Hercules, was coming down the stairs from the second floor. He glanced over at us and almost seemed to roll his green eyes. Then he headed for the kitchen with a flick of his tail. Hercules was indifferent—or maybe disdainful would be a better word—to the joys of catnip.

I picked up Owen and set him on the floor. He stretched, yawned and began to wash his face. The effort was a little slap-dash. I went out to the kitchen and dumped the yellow feather and the chicken head in the garbage can. Then I picked up the decapitated corpse and tossed that in, too. There were bits of dried catnip spread across the floor, a pretty common occur-rence in this house. There was no sign of Hercules, which likely meant he was out in the porch, looking through the win-dow, his way of communing with nature. For the most part, Hercules liked *outside* best when he was looking at it from *inside*.

Hercules and Owen had been tiny, feral kittens when I'd found them, out at Wisteria Hill, the former Henderson home-stead, about a month after I'd arrived in town. They were so small and so determined to come with me, in the end I'd brought them home. Both cats were affectionate with me, but wouldn't allow anyone else to touch them. Any attempt at all ended with claws and yowling—the latter not always from one of the cats. So I had ended up with two roommates that had strong opinions on pizza toppings, catnip and Barry Manilow.

I got the broom and the dustpan and swept up the bits of catnip. Then I went upstairs to finish getting ready for work. When I came back down again Owen was in the kitchen trying to pull open the basement door with a paw. Before I left for work I would leave it slightly ajar for him. The basement was where he kept his stash of catnip chickens and frogs, among other things. It was the cat equivalent to the Batcave.

I opened the door for him, and he meowed a thank-you as he started down the steps.

"No more chickens or frogs up here," I warned.

His response was to flick his tail at me. I knew what gesture *that* was the cat equivalent to. Then he disappeared. Not just into the darkness of the basement. He literally disappeared. As improbable as it seemed, Owen had the ability to vanish at will, usually when it was most likely to complicate my life. Which, it sometimes seemed, was why he did it.

Owen—and Hercules—were no ordinary cats. Owen could disappear. Vanish. Hercules couldn't, but he could walk through walls. Brick walls, stone walls, walls made of wood and drywall; none of them could stop him. I had no idea where either of their abilities came from, although I'd spent a lot of time looking for answers.

It wasn't the kind of thing I could talk to anyone about. I'd tried to imagine asking my friend Roma, who was also the boys' vet, "Do any of the cats at your clinic become invisible? Can any of them walk through walls?" At best I'd end up somewhere having my head examined. At worst Owen and Hercules would. In the beginning I'd kept hoping I'd discover some reasonable explanation. Maybe it was some kind of genetic mutation. Then to my surprise, slowly over time, I'd gotten used to the cats' skills. More than once they'd even proved useful.

I put on my shoes and jacket and grabbed my messenger bag. As I'd suspected, Hercules was in the porch, sitting on the bench, looking out the window. I stopped to give him a scratch on the top of his head. "Have a good day," I said.

"Mrrr," he replied, which I took to mean, "You too."

It was a beautiful, sunny morning, especially welcome after two straight days of rain. I headed down Mountain Road toward the library. The street gradually turned in toward the center of town as it got closer to the water and the roofline of the library building came into view. The Mayville Heights Free Public Library had been built near the center of a curve of shoreline and was protected from the water by a high rock wall. It was a Carnegie library, built with money donated by industrialist and philanthropist Andrew Carnegie. The two-story brick building was topped with a copper-roofed cupola that was just beginning to develop the distinctive green patina.

As much as I loved the library, for me, one of the best parts of Mayville Heights was the riverfront. There were beautiful old buildings like the library and the Stratton Theatre. Huge elm and black walnut trees lined the walking trail that led from the old warehouses out at the point, past the downtown businesses, all the way out beyond the marina to Wild Rose Bluff. You could still see the barges and boats go by on the water the way they had more than a hundred years ago.

I parked my truck at the far end of the library parking lot

and walked over to the front door, looking over the outside of the building the way I always did. The library had been renovated and updated to celebrate its centenary several years ago, which was why I'd first come to Mayville Heights. I'd been hired to supervise the restoration work and I had only planned to stay until the project was finished, but I had fallen in love with the town and the people and eventually with one person in particular: Detective Marcus Gordon, who I was going to marry in less than two months. We'd spent an hour the previous night trying cake samples with my friend Georgia, who owned Sweet Things bakery. I had no idea how we were going to pick a wedding cake flavor. Everything Georgia made was delicious.

I turned off the alarm and unlocked the main doors to the library. Then I stepped into the building, turning as I did so to look up above the entrance. A carved wooden sun, three feet across, hung there. Above it were stenciled the words LET THERE BE LIGHT. That same inscription was over the door of the first Carnegie library in Dunfermline, Scotland. The sun had been made by Oren Kenyon, a talented carpenter and musician, who had worked on the building's restoration.

I had some time before we opened for the day, so I decided to make coffee and try just a bite or two of a couple of the cake samples that Georgia had sent home with me. Maybe that would help me narrow down the choices. I'd put three of the little cupcakes in with my lunch the night before and Marcus had teased that it was just my way of rationalizing eating cake for breakfast.

"I'm not rationalizing anything," I'd told him, as I set the cupcakes on the counter beside my lunchbox—a vintage 1960s metal Batman and Robin lunchbox—which had been a Christmas gift from my sister, Sarah. "This is legitimate research. And as a librarian, meticulous research is important to me. Plus they're for lunch, not breakfast." I'd squared my shoulders, clasped my hands in front of me and tried to look serious.

It hadn't worked.

Marcus had caught my arm and pulled me toward him. Laughing, he'd kissed the top of my head and said, "Research. Right. You keep telling yourself that, Kathleen."

I was about to head up to the second-floor staff room when I saw a faint glimmer of light out of the corner of my eye. I stopped in my tracks. Where was it coming from? I knew there had been no lights left on in the building the night before because Marcus and I had stopped in after the cake testing. I had wanted to check on the book drop. It had been jamming half-shut in the past few days. I had ended up being the last person out of the building. I'd walked around the main floor the way I always did before I locked up, checking to make sure that there was no one still inside, no lights were left on and nothing was out of place. Somehow, I seemed to have missed . . . something.

I switched on the overhead lights and looked around. And then I saw it. I pressed a hand to my chest as my heart began to pound in shock. About twenty feet away from me, in front of a display of new nonfiction books, a body was slumped on the mosaic tile floor. Several of the books had been knocked over and a painting on the wall above the wooden bookshelves was hanging askew. A small flashlight lay about a foot away from the body, next to a pair of needle-nose pliers and a black-handled pocketknife. The flashlight's faint beam was what had caught my attention.

I hurried across the room and crouched down next to the body. To my shock I realized I recognized the person. My stomach lurched and for a moment I couldn't breathe.

It was Will Redfern. His hair was shorter than the last time I'd seen him and flecked with gray now, but it was Will.

I felt for a pulse at his neck with a shaking hand. I couldn't find one. The body was cold and stiff. There was a small stain on his dark sweatshirt that might have been blood, and some kind of injury to his head. Will was definitely dead.

I sat back on my heels and closed my eyes for a moment, pressing one hand to the top of my head. What was Will Redfern doing in my library? He had been the original contractor for the building's renovations. He'd been arrested for assaulting me before the job was finished and ended up in jail. As far as I knew, he'd just gotten out a couple of weeks ago. Will had shown up yesterday, wanting to talk to me, but I had been out of the building. Now, less than twenty-four hours later, he was dead.

I took a couple of deep breaths to steady myself. Then I got to my feet and called 911. I didn't call Marcus because I knew he was in court first thing today. I waited by the front door and avoided looking back at the body.

Officer Stephen Keller was the first person to arrive. He was former military, square jawed and square shouldered. We had met at crime scenes before. I showed him where the body was and then stayed out of his way.

Like I had, Officer Keller checked for a pulse. I was guessing he'd also taken note of the gash on the side of Will's head the same way I had. He looked at the floor around the body then straightened up and did a quick survey of the space.

"Is anyone else here besides you, Ms. Paulson?" he asked.

I shook my head. I explained how I'd first glimpsed the faint beam from the flashlight and then found Will's body.

"Do you know this man?"

"Yes," I said. I swallowed down the sour taste of bile at the back of my throat. Stephen Keller had arrived in Mayville Heights after Will had been sent to jail so he wouldn't have recognized him. I explained who Will was and how I knew him.

"Is there any reason you can think of for Mr. Redfern to be in the building?" Officer Keller asked.

I couldn't think of any good one. "No," I said. "The doors were locked. The alarm was on. I don't understand how he got inside without triggering it."

He nodded. "Ms. Paulson, you know the procedure."

I nodded. I knew it too well. I gestured at the checkout desk. "I'll just stay right here."

"Thank you," he said. He stepped away to call for more assistance.

I leaned against the front desk. I set my messenger bag on top of it and took a sip of my coffee, wrapping both hands around the metal travel mug as Marcus came through the door.

I stared at him in surprise. "What are you doing here?" I asked. "I thought you were in court this morning."

"The guy changed his plea at the last minute." He was talking to me, but his gaze had shifted in the direction of Officer Keller and Will Redfern's body. Marcus held up one finger, letting the officer know he'd be there in a minute. Finally, he turned his full attention to me. "Are you all right?" he asked. He was wearing a dark blue suit with a pale gray shirt and a blue patterned tie loose at his neck.

"I'm fine," I said. I cleared my throat. "Marcus, that's . . . that's Will Redfern over there. He's dead."

He stared at me for along moment. "Are you certain?" he finally said.

I nodded.

He exhaled loudly. "Just . . . just stay here, okay? I'll be right back." He walked over to Officer Keller. The younger man said something, gesturing with one hand. Marcus nodded and then he crouched down to get a good look at the body. He didn't bother checking for a pulse but I saw him lean closer for a better look at the injury to the side of Will's head before he stood up again.

I started making a mental list of all the people, beyond staff, whom I needed to let know the library was going to be closed for a while because it clearly *was* going to be shut down for at least the next couple of days. I had no idea how Will had gotten into the building, what he'd been doing here, or what had happened to him, but that injury to the side of his head didn't look like an accident to me. Neither did the blood on his sweatshirt. My library was a crime scene.

Marcus had gotten to his feet, and he walked back over to me. "Kathleen, do you have any idea what Will was doing in the building?" he asked.

"I don't," I said. I folded one arm around my midsection. "It doesn't make any sense."

He raked a hand back through his dark, wavy hair the way he always did when he was a bit stressed. "Okay. Tell me what happened. Start at the beginning."

"There's not much to tell. I got here early. The alarm was working, and the door was locked. I didn't notice anything that seemed off to me. I came inside and I was about to head upstairs to start the coffee when I saw a light, very dim, out of the corner of my eye."

"The flashlight," he said.

I nodded and took another sip of my coffee. "I put on the overhead lights and that's when I saw the body." I explained how I'd gone to check for a pulse and then realized it was Will Redfern lying there.

"Is there any way Will could have gotten the alarm code?"

"I don't see how. It's reset regularly and there are only a

handful of people who know the code at any given time, and I trust all of them."

Marcus looked over at the main doors for a moment before turning back to me. He was already in what I thought of as police officer mode, looking at everything and gathering facts, filing everything away in his head. "Could Will have kept a key to the building?" he asked.

"It wouldn't matter if he had," I said. "Harry changed all the locks before Will went to jail." Harry Taylor, who took care of all the maintenance at the library, had recently suggested we change to electronic locks on the building. It occurred to me that maybe that was something I should bring up at the next library board meeting.

"Could he have gotten a key or copied one somehow?"

I hesitated. "Maybe. I can't say for sure. You and I both know that Will has . . . had some less than stellar connections. I wouldn't be surprised to find out that he knew someone who could have helped him get into the building."

Marcus nodded. "Yeah, I know." He turned to look at the body again.

Officer Keller caught his eye and motioned him over.

"I'm sorry," Marcus said. "Just give me a minute."

"It's all right," I told him. "You have a job to do. Is it all right if I call Susan and Abigail and tell them not to come in?"

He thought for a moment, then nodded. "Go ahead, but for now can you just say there was a break-in?"

I took another sip of my coffee and set the mug on the

counter beside me. "I'll do that, but you know that won't hold off the gossip for very long."

He blew out a breath. "I know," he said.

I called Susan and Abigail, who had the morning shifts, and told them the agreed-upon story. "They didn't take the computers, did they?" Susan asked.

I glanced over my shoulder, just to be certain, but our new computers were all there. "The computers are fine," I said. "I'll let you know as soon as I find out when we can open."

I sent a text to Mary, who was scheduled to come in after lunch, to let her know what was going on and sent another one to our part-time student, Levi. Then I called Lita to tell her I'd be late for our meeting. I had budget estimates to drop off to her and I could see it was going to be a while before I got out of the building.

Lita was Everett Henderson's assistant. Everett was the chairperson of the library board. He'd paid for the renovations to the library, his gift to the town for the building's centennial. He'd also hired me.

"Just come whenever," Lita said. She paused for a moment. "Are you all right?"

Had something in my voice given me away? "I'm fine," I said. "I'll see you soon."

I went behind the desk and found a black marker and a roll of packing tape. I fished a large piece of cardboard out of the recycling bin and I made a sign for the front door to tell our patrons the building would be closed for the day "due to unforeseen circumstances." Once people saw the medical examiner's van parked outside, the whole town would know more than just a break-in had happened.

Eventually the van did arrive, and Marcus joined me again. I averted my eyes as Will's body was wheeled past us. Even so I felt a twinge of sadness. I hadn't liked Will. He had been difficult to work with—unscrupulous, lazy, and he stretched the truth until it snapped like an overtightened guitar string. But no matter what he had done, he didn't deserve to have his life end like this.

"Because I could not stop for death— He kindly stopped for me," I said softly.

Marcus raised a questioning eyebrow at me.

"Emily Dickinson," I said. I looked around as if I could somehow find an answer to what had happened. Why had Will Redfern been in the library and had it somehow gotten him killed?

chapter 2

Once Will's body had been removed from the building, I turned to Marcus. "You saw the pocketknife and the pliers on the floor, obviously," I said.

He nodded. "I saw them."

I rubbed the space between my eyebrows with two fingers. "I don't want to jump to conclusions just because . . . just because it was Will, and I know it doesn't make any sense, but it looks as though he was trying to take the painting that's hanging on the wall over there." I gestured toward the bookcase Will's body had been lying in front of.

"Show me," Marcus said.

We walked over to where a crime scene technician was taking photographs, standing far enough back not to get in the way.

"Do you mean that painting?" Marcus asked, pointing at the small watercolor, which was still hanging sideways on the wall above the shelves.

I nodded. "That's the one."

"Is it worth anything?" he asked.

I studied the picture—a lemon tree next to a small, sun-dappled building—for a moment. "I don't think so. You should probably talk to Susan to be certain," I said, "but as far as I know that painting was donated for the yard sale that we had right after the renovations were finished. So that's about five years ago. I held back a few pieces of artwork—some paintings and some posters—that came in because I thought the walls looked a little bare in here." I had decided to keep this particular painting because it had reminded me of one painted by John Singer Sargent that I had seen in the Museum of Fine Arts in Boston.

"How long has it been hanging there?" Marcus asked. "I don't remember seeing it there before."

"It's just been there a few days. I got Harry to put it up the end of last week." I watched the tech move in closer to take a photo of the painting. To me it looked as though Will—or someone—had tried to wrench it from the wall when they couldn't easily lift it down. "I'd been switching the artwork out myself fairly regularly until that piece got taken a couple of weeks ago." Someone had lifted a small oil painting off the wall in the reference section and managed to walk out of the building with it. Whoever it was hadn't left any clues.

"I'm sorry we couldn't find the person, or the picture." He folded his arms and studied the painting.

I shrugged. "That's okay. I didn't really expect you would. And I know that painting definitely wasn't worth very much. It was done by Jon Bell years ago." Jon owned a camera store and photography business here in town. "Even so, given what happened, Harry decided we needed a more secure way of putting things up. So he's been rehanging everything, a few pieces at a time, using this locking screw system he found. It requires a special little T-shaped tool to get a picture down." I gestured at the lopsided painting. "I'm guessing that's why that's still on the wall."

Marcus looked all around the main floor. I couldn't see any other piece of artwork that had been tampered with, but I knew the police would check the whole library.

"So none of the art in the building is valuable?" he said. We started back over to the circulation desk.

"To the best of my knowledge, no," I said. I pointed to several small bird paintings that I had hung near the main entrance. "Those ones for instance are just from a paint-by-numbers kit. You could talk to Mary or Susan. They've been here a lot longer than I have. I just don't see how we could have anything that has more than aesthetic value. Or that just makes people smile."

Marcus pulled his tie loose and stuffed it in his pocket. "We don't know for sure that Will was trying to steal that painting. But I think it wouldn't hurt to have it examined by someone with some expertise, just to be certain."

It didn't make any sense to me that Will had broken into the library to steal that watercolor. But then it didn't make any sense that he had broken into the building at all. "Well, you could talk to Ruby," I said.

Ruby Blackthorne was the president of the artists' co-op and she volunteered with our Reading Buddies program. She was a talented photographer and created huge pop art paintings among other things. "I know Ruby studied art history in college and if she can't tell you anything about that painting she should know of someone who can."

"Yeah, that's a good idea," Marcus said. He seemed distracted. His gaze drifted over to the painting.

I touched his arm. "Is it all right if I leave now?" I asked.

He focused on me again. "Go ahead. I know that it's pretty much impossible to keep what happened here quiet for long, but for now, could you please stick with the break-in story? It's true. It's not just the whole truth."

"I can do that," I said. "I'm not going to get my building back at the end of the day, am I?"

Marcus swiped a hand across his face. "I'm sorry, Kathleen," he said. "I just don't see that happening."

I looked around. A lot of people in town depended on the library for their entertainment, for our public access computers, for the various programs we ran, for the chance just to be around other people for a little while. For some of them, the building being closed would be a hardship.

"It can't be helped," I said. "I'll leave the sign up for today and come put up a new one tomorrow. If you need me, I'm going for a short meeting with Lita and then I'm going home."

He nodded. "I might have a few more questions for you later. Either way I'll call you at some point." He gave my hand a squeeze and headed back to where Will's body had been lying.

I picked up my coffee mug and my bag and went out to the truck. I slid behind the wheel, dumped everything on the passenger side and then slumped against the back of the seat.

Will Redfern was dead.

Dead.

It didn't feel real. He'd been gone for several years, and according to town gossip, showed up in Mayville Heights just a few days ago. Now Will was dead. What had he been doing in the library? Had he really been trying to steal that painting? Why on earth would he have wanted it?

I remembered that injury to the side of his head. I had no medical training beyond basic first aid but I couldn't figure out how Will had hit his head. There was nothing in the vicinity of his body that could have caused that wound as far as I had seen. And that stain on his shirt that I was pretty certain was blood. What had caused that? However Will Redfern had died, it didn't look as though it was accidental to me.

I drove over to Henderson Holdings. Lita was just making a fresh pot of coffee when I walked in. She looked at me and raised her eyebrows. "Yes, please," I said, dropping into a chair.

"I figured you might like a cup," Lita said as she poured. Something about the way she looked at me told me that she knew what was really going on at the library, but she didn't ask me any questions so I didn't have to hedge any answers.

I gave her the estimates I'd worked on and we talked about the proposed budget and the upcoming library board meeting. I shared some of my tentative plans for the coming year. Lita made notes. "I'll get this all back to you by the end of the week," she said when we were finally finished.

"That's lots of time," I said. "Thank you."

Lita set her pen down on the desk. "Kathleen, you see Riley fairly regularly, don't you?" she asked.

I nodded. "She comes into the library pretty much every week." Riley Hollister and her little brother, Duncan, were living with Lita while their father, Lonnie, was in rehab. Riley and I shared a love of math and books.

"How does she seem to you?"

"She's doing better in school. She pretends she doesn't really care about grades but she does. And she likes being at the clinic. Roma says she's great with the animals and their owners." Riley was volunteering at Roma's veterinarian practice.

Lita smiled then. "I admit I was a bit surprised to hear she

20

was relating to people almost as well as she does to the animals."

"Riley can be prickly but she has a good heart," I said. "So why are you asking about her? Is something going on?"

Her smile faded. "Yes. It doesn't look like Lonnie will be coming back."

"He's not coming back soon or he's not coming back at all?"

"Probably not at all. You know Lonnie isn't capable of raising the kids without a support system and that support system is here. But he won't stay sober if he comes back, and let's face it, Lonnie is a lot better off when he's away from his father's influence."

I nodded. The elder Hollister wasn't someone I liked.

Lita picked up the cup of coffee she'd poured for herself and then set it back down again. "Riley and Duncan living with me was only supposed to be temporary. Don't get me wrong, I don't have a problem keeping them with me and raising them both if that's what they need, but I want to be sure *I'm* what they need. I want them to be happy."

"I think they are happy," I said. "You know they have a lot better life with you than they did out at the farm with Lonnie and Gerald."

Lita laughed. "That's a very low bar, Kathleen." Her expression grew serious again. "I'm not ready for a rocking chair on the front porch but I'm not a kid, either. I want Riley and Duncan to have a home that's here for them now and twenty years from now."

"Maybe a home for now is enough for now," I said.

She shot me a look. "You sound like Burtis."

Burtis Chapman was Lita's gentleman friend. She didn't like the term "boyfriend." Burtis had suggested "boy toy." That hadn't gotten an enthusiastic response, either.

I smiled. "Burtis is a very smart man with excellent taste in lady friends. You could do worse than listening to him."

I asked Lita to keep me updated on Lonnie's situation and she promised she would.

"When will the building be open again?" she asked as I stood up and slipped on my jacket. I didn't get the sense that she was fishing for information. Not that she needed to. Lita was related to half the town on her mother's side of the family and the other half thanks to her father. She knew everyone, and as a result she also knew everything that was going on.

"By Friday, I hope," I said, holding up my crossed fingers.

"Let us know if you need anything," she said. I promised I would, thanked her again and left.

When I got home Hercules was sitting on one of the Adirondack chairs in the backyard. He started at the sight of me. I walked across the grass and dropped into the chair next to him. He meowed and gave me a quizzical look, green eyes narrowed.

"Do you remember Will Redfern?" I asked.

The cat wrinkled his whiskers at me.

22

I decided to take that as a yes. "Well, it seems he broke into the library and . . . and well, he's dead," I said.

Will's death bothered me. He'd been given more than one second chance that I knew of, and it didn't seem like he'd taken advantage of any of them. Even so, he didn't deserve to be left to die, alone, on the floor in the library.

Hercules butted my hand with his head and I stroked his fur. He began to purr. After a minute or so I picked him up and headed for the house, stopping to get my messenger bag and my mug from the stoop where I had left them.

Owen was in the kitchen sitting at the table. He seemed startled to see me as well. There was something on the chair he was seated on. I set Hercules on the floor. The two of them exchanged a look.

"I do live here, you know," I said.

"Merow," Hercules said, blinking his green eyes at me. I saw another look pass between them. I had the feeling they were humoring me.

"What do you have there?" I said to Owen.

He gazed up at me with his best "Who, me?" expression. And he moved one paw on top of whatever was resting on the chair.

"Let me see," I said. I set my bag and my travel mug on the chair next to him.

He put a second paw beside the first one. His chin came up and his look changed to one of defiance. So this was how it was going to go.

I looked up at the kitchen ceiling, feigned surprise and said, "Good heavens, where did that come from?"

Owen immediately looked up. I grabbed the edge of what he had been trying to hide with his paws and yanked it away from him. He yowled indignantly.

I shrugged one shoulder. "Don't get all huffy because you always fall for that."

I looked down at Hercules, who was looking a little smug, unblinkingly eyeing his brother. "And don't you act so superior," I told the little tuxedo cat. "I saw you look up as well." He dropped his head and suddenly got very interested in washing his left paw.

Owen had been hiding a black-and-white photo-booth picture that had been stuck to my refrigerator with a small magnet. It was a photo of my friend Maggie, whom Owen adored. I looked over at the fridge. The cat's paw magnet that had been holding the picture in place was still there, slightly skewed to one side.

"How did you get that photo?" I asked. I had no idea he could leap that high. Owen looked past me as though I wasn't even in the room and jumped down to the floor. Then he disappeared. Literally. It was his way of having the last word.

I put Maggie's photo back on the refrigerator. Then I hung up my jacket, put my shoes on the mat, and set my mug in the sink.

I made a pot of coffee because my brain ran better when it

was fully caffeinated. I ate two of the tiny cupcakes I had packed to take to work and decided I liked the chocolate just a bit more than the spice cake. I gave Hercules two sardine crackers. He seemed to like both of them equally well.

Hercules trailed me upstairs, poking his head in the closet while I changed into jeans and a long-sleeved T-shirt. Then he followed me into the bathroom, sitting on the top of the toilet tank while I cleaned and then vacuumed two cats' worth of hair from the floor.

I was halfway under the bed with the vacuum, chasing a clump of cat hair the size of a small tumbleweed, when my phone rang. It was Marcus. I sat on the floor to answer.

"I just wanted to let you know that the library will be closed for another day but I'm hoping you can have the building back sometime on Friday."

"Thank you," I said. "Will you be able to make it for supper tonight?"

"I think so," he said.

I pictured him standing in the hallway at the police station, which was where he usually went to call me.

"I talked to Ruby. She's going to meet me first thing in the morning at the library. Could you be there as well? She might have questions about that painting that I can't answer but you can."

"I can be there," I said. "Like I said, I'll need to put a new sign on the door."

"I've gotta go," Marcus said. He promised he'd let me know if he couldn't make supper and we said good-bye.

Hercules padded over to me. He'd been in the closet, probably rearranging my shoes. He climbed onto my lap and looked up at me. "What the heck was Will Redfern doing at the library trying to steal a painting?" I asked him. "Is it possible that somehow it actually is worth money or was Will trying to cover up something else he was there to do?"

Hercules made a face. He didn't seem to have any more idea than I did.

I was the first person to arrive at the library in the morning. I'd brought a new sign and a roll of zebra-striped duct tape to attach it to the door. Ruby showed up just as I was tearing off the last piece of tape.

"Hi, Kathleen," she said as she came up the stairs. "I didn't know you were going to be here."

Ruby Blackthorne was about my height, five six or so. She was generally dressed in jeans and a T-shirt with some kind of saying on the front. Today's had a line drawing of a haggard-looking hamster with a caption that read: ***First I Drink the Coffee. Then I Do the Things***. She also had multiple piercings in both ears and her hair was generally some color other than her natural brown. At the moment it was a soft shade of lavender that went well with her fair skin.

I turned to smile at her. "Marcus thought you might have

some questions that he couldn't answer but I might be able to," I said.

"I have one," she said. "Do you have any idea where the painting came from?"

I shook my head. "All I can tell you is that it was donated for that yard sale we had right after the renovations."

"I remember that. You were trying to come up with some money to start Reading Buddies."

"That's right."

Ruby frowned. "So the painting has been at the library for years. Why didn't I notice it before? I thought I'd seen every piece of artwork you have in the building."

"Probably because it spent most of the time in a box on a shelf in the workroom," I said a little sheepishly. "There were four or five paintings and a few posters that I forgot all about. I just came across them a couple of weeks ago. As for the painting, Susan might be able to tell you more about who donated it. She organized that sale."

"Good idea. I'll talk to her," Ruby said. Her smile faded. "Marcus told me that Will Redfern is dead."

I slipped my bag off of my shoulder and set it at my feet, to buy a little time as much as anything. "Will was far from someone I liked," I finally said, "but I never would have wished for anything like this to happen to him."

"That's because you're a much nicer person than I am," Ruby said flatly. "He broke your wrist, he could have done worse, and he almost got away with it."

"But in the end he didn't. He went to jail."

Ruby gave a snort of derision. "And I'm willing to bet he didn't learn anything from that whole experience."

Marcus drove into the parking lot then, which meant I didn't have to say that I had a feeling she was probably right.

I let us into the building and turned on the overhead lights. Marcus took Ruby over to the painting and I followed.

"Is it all right if I get a little closer?" she asked.

"Go ahead," Marcus said.

She studied the picture for what felt like a full minute, a frown creasing her forehead. Marcus and I waited without speaking. Finally, Ruby turned to face us. Her expression was a mix of surprise and elation. "This is going to sound crazy but I'm almost certain this is a very valuable piece of art. What I can't figure out is what the heck it's doing here."

"What do you mean by valuable?" Marcus asked. His gaze went from Ruby to the painting behind her. He looked confused.

"More than a million dollars, give or take," Ruby said.

"For that little painting?" I said. "I don't understand."

Ruby nodded. "I'm about ninety-nine percent certain it was stolen as part of the Hamilton art heist about six years ago."

"That sounds familiar," Marcus said. "But I don't remember the details."

Ruby glanced at the painting again before turning her attention to Marcus. "A businessman by the name of Robert Hamilton was loaning some of his very extensive collection of artwork to the Museum of Art and Culture. Several paintings were stolen from his home the day before they were to be transferred to the museum. Hamilton eventually got almost all of the paintings back, but the thieves were never caught."

Marcus was nodding as though Ruby had jogged his memory.

"Almost all of the paintings?" I said.

Ruby looked over her shoulder at the watercolor again. "All but one small watercolor."

"This one," I said.

She nodded. "I think so."

Marcus shook his head. "I don't mean to sound skeptical or doubt your expertise, but do you really think this is the missing painting? How did it end up here?"

Ruby shrugged. "I'm as sure as I can be. I'm no expert, but I feel certain this is the missing painting." She tapped her chest with one hand as if to emphasize her certainty. "There was a lot of media coverage about the theft at the time and I read and watched everything I could find. I admit I'm fascinated by this kind of thing. The Isabella Stewart Gardner Museum heist. Montreal Museum of Fine Arts break-in. Did you know that the *Mona Lisa* was stolen back in 1911?"

Marcus shook his head and I nodded.

Ruby pulled out her phone. "Give me a minute," she said. "I might be able to find one of the articles about the theft with an image of this painting." After tapping the screen multiple times, she turned the phone around.

I looked carefully at the image and then back at the picture on the wall. I had no art training like Ruby, but it looked like the same painting to me.

"I see what you mean," Marcus said. He looked up from the phone. "They look the same. Would you send me this link, please?"

Ruby nodded and turned the phone back around. "You need an expert to be certain. In theory, this could be a good forgery. But if it's real, the bigger question is how did it end up here in the library?"

"And how is Will connected to the painting?" I said. "Did he somehow recognize it?"

Ruby laughed. "Yeah, I don't see how Will Redfern, of all people, could have recognized that painting. C'mon, Kathleen. Are you trying to say he was some kind of art connoisseur?"

I shook my head. "No, I don't see Will as some kind of art lover." I held up a hand. "But he was here in the building the day before he died. I didn't see him or talk to him, but Mary did."

Ruby's eyes narrowed. "What did he want?" she asked.

"According to Mary he wanted to know if I would be open to talking to him. He claimed he was trying to clean up all the messes he'd left behind."

"You weren't going to say yes, were you?"

"I was thinking about it."

Ruby closed her eyes and shook her head, a wry smile twisting her mouth.

Out of the corner of my eye I saw Marcus's shoulders tighten. He hadn't liked my decision, either.

"It would have been a yes with conditions," I said. "I was willing to talk to Will, but in a public space, with other people around." I stared past Ruby for a moment, remembering how I'd struggled with the decision. "I told Mary that maybe he'd changed. She said a leopard doesn't change its spots."

I remembered how Mary had looked, standing by the circulation desk in a green cardigan covered with yellow and red tulips, her annoyance with me showing in the jut of her chin and the set of her shoulders. "Don't give Will any kind of absolution, Kathleen," she'd said firmly. "He doesn't deserve to be let off the hook. He hasn't earned it. He had that same cat-that-swallowed-the-canary expression on his face that he always used to have when he thought he was getting away with something. Don't be a fool."

"Mary was right," Ruby said. She gestured at the painting. "The fact that he might have been in the building to try to steal something just proves it. But still, he didn't deserve to be killed." She looked at Marcus. "I'm guessing that's what happened and Will didn't actually have the big one while he was trying to get that painting off the wall."

"No comment," Marcus said with a hint of a smile.

Ruby smiled back at him. "I can send you several names of people who can tell you definitively whether or not that's the stolen painting."

"I'd appreciate that," he said.

"I should be able to get them for you by this afternoon. I just have to make sure a couple of them are in the country." She tipped her head to one side and raised her eyebrows at him. "And I know to keep this whole conversation to myself."

"I'd appreciate that, too," Marcus said, and his smile got a little bit bigger.

Ruby gave me a hug. "I'll see you at class tonight," she said.

I smiled. "Thanks for helping."

Once Ruby was gone I let out a sigh. "None of this makes any sense," I told Marcus. "How did a stolen painting end up in my library and why on earth was Will Redfern of all people trying to steal it?"

Marcus put his hands on my shoulders. "Look, we don't know yet that it is the missing painting. And we don't know for sure that Will was trying to steal it."

"Fair enough," I said. "But we do know someone killed Will." I waited without speaking and finally he gave a slight nod.

I felt my heart sink. Someone had killed Will Redfern. Who and why?

chapter 3

I spent the afternoon working from home, catching up on paperwork. I had a big bowl of tortellini and sausage soup for supper and then headed down to tai chi class. Ruby was sitting on the bench at the top of the stairs changing her shoes when I got there.

"I sent those names to Marcus this afternoon," she said.

"Thank you," I said, sitting down next to her to change my own footwear.

"And I owe you an apology."

I turned to look at her. Her lavender-colored hair was pulled up into two stubby pigtails that stuck straight out on each side of her head. "For what?" I asked.

Ruby looked down at the floor for a moment, then her eyes met mine. "You were willing to give Will a second chance. Just because I don't think he deserved it doesn't mean I should have criticized your decision. One of the things I like about you is your faith in people. I don't always share it, but it is a good thing. So, I'm sorry."

"You're not the only one who questioned my decision, including a couple of furry critics."

Ruby smiled. "Those cats of yours are pretty smart."

I smiled back at her. "Your heart was in the right place. You don't need to apologize."

Ruby waited while I slipped on my tai chi shoes and we walked into the studio together. Roma was standing by the window, working on part of the form: my nemesis, Cloud Hands, to be exact.

"I need to talk to Roma," Ruby said. "Tell Marcus to call me if he has any questions."

"I will," I said. I walked over to the tea table where Maggie was standing. Maggie was the first real friend I'd made in Mayville Heights. We had bonded over our shared love of the cheesy reality show *Gotta Dance*. I would always be grateful that I'd accepted Rebecca's invitation to try her tai chi class. I wasn't so sure that Marcus and I would have ended up with each other if it hadn't been for Maggie and Roma all but physically pushing the two of us together.

"I have a question," I said. "What can you tell me about the theft of artwork belonging to a man named Robert Hamilton about six years ago?"

Maggie was tall and slender in gray leggings and a bright yellow T-shirt. She had curly blond hair, cropped close to her head, and green eyes. She smiled at me over the top of her cup. The tea she'd made smelled like peppermint and vanilla. I liked the aroma of the various teas Maggie drank, but I was a die-hard coffee lover.

"I can tell you that the value of the paintings stolen was in the millions of dollars and Robert Hamilton managed to regain all of them but one. How exactly he did that no one seems to know."

"But there's been some speculation."

She took a sip of her tea and nodded. "Quite a lot of it over the years. The general consensus is that he used money and possibly a little bribery to get his artwork back." She set her cup on the table. "One of the most interesting things about the whole thing, at least to me, is that the thief or thieves took the most significant pieces of artwork in the collection. In other words, they knew what was valuable and what other collectors might be looking for."

"So they knew they could find buyers who wouldn't care that the paintings were stolen."

"I think so. This has something to do with you finding Will Redfern's body at the library, doesn't it?"

I hesitated.

"Kathleen, I know Marcus is trying to keep it quiet, but the whole town knows what happened," Maggie said. "You know that any day now Bridget's going to have the story splashed all over the paper."

Bridget Lowe was the publisher of the *Mayville Heights Chronicle*. It was one of the few small papers in the state still in the black. She prided herself on ferreting out stories ahead of other news media.

"It might, *might* have something to do with Will," I finally said, "but please, Mags, keep that to yourself."

Maggie nodded. "Of course I will, but you know if Bridget finds out it'll be in the next edition of the paper."

"I know," I said. "So let's hope she doesn't anytime soon. It makes it difficult for Marcus to build a case when Bridget is putting every detail on the front page of the paper."

Roma joined us then. "The package will be on time," she told Maggie. I saw her gaze flick sideways to me for a moment.

"Perfect," Maggie said. They grinned at each other.

"What package?" I asked.

The two of them exchanged a look and then in unison mimed zipping their mouths, closing a lock and hiding the key in their shoes.

"Does this package have anything to do with the shower this weekend?"

Maggie and Roma were hosting a wedding shower for me on Sunday. I hadn't been able to get a single detail about what they had planned from either one of them.

"You're wasting your time asking questions," Roma said.

She tucked a strand of dark hair behind her ears. "We're not telling you anything." She gave me a big and very insincere smile and mischief sparkled in her brown eyes. "All you need to do is be ready when Maggie comes to pick you up on Sunday."

"You could at least give me a hint about what we're going to do. I don't even know what to wear."

"Owen will help you pick something," Maggie said, her voice matter-of-fact. Since Owen often seemed to have an opinion on what clothing I chose, it wasn't beyond the realm of possibility.

I had no idea what they had planned, but I was touched that both of them had put so much work into this celebration for me. "I love you both," I said, suddenly overcome with a rush of emotion.

"We love you, too," Roma said. She wrapped me in a hug.

Maggie reached across the table, caught my hand and gave it a squeeze. "I always knew you and Marcus were right for each other."

"How could you? I didn't even know that," I said.

Roma laughed. "I know. That's why we had to give the two of you a little nudge."

I remembered how Maggie had set up Marcus and me so we ended up sitting next to each other at the summer music festival and how Roma had put us together to feed the feral cats out at Wisteria Hill long before she owned the property.

Roma looked at Maggie. "Maybe we could be professional matchmakers, you know, as a sideline."

Maggie nodded. "I've always thought that Ruby and Harry would make a good couple."

"Harry Taylor is old enough to be Ruby's father," I said. I was pretty sure Maggie was just messing with me.

"Ruby's an old soul," Roma said. "And Harry's young at heart. I think they'd work."

"Harry does like to cook," Maggie added. "And Ruby likes to eat."

They were definitely messing with me. I looked at my watch. "Isn't it time for class?" I asked.

"It is," Maggie said. She took a couple of steps forward, clapped her hands and called, "Circle, everyone." Then she looked back over her shoulder, smiled cheekily at me and said, "We'll talk later."

Maggie worked us hard and my shirt was damp with sweat by the time the class finished. I went home and made my usual after-class snack of hot chocolate and peanut butter toast. I sat at the table and pulled my computer closer. Hercules landed on my lap and looked from me to the screen.

"Hello," I said. Hercules seemed to like helping me research things and more than once he'd "accidentally" clicked on something that had ended up assisting my investigation.

We looked at images of the stolen paintings from the Hamilton heist. I was convinced that Ruby was right about the painting at the library. It was locked away at the police station now, for safekeeping.

"What do you think?" I asked Hercules.

He leaned in closer to the computer and seemed to study the image on the screen. For all I knew he really was.

"Merow," he said after a moment. He looked at me.

"Yeah, I think it is, too," I said.

I couldn't find a lot of information online about Robert Hamilton. Everyone did seem to agree that he was crazy smart. Hamilton was a self-made man from a blue-collar family who owned a company that made medical equipment. He had invented an incredibly small camera, used in brain surgery, which allowed surgeons to remove complex tumors that before his camera were considered inoperable. Hamilton's company was also considered a pioneer in virtual reality surgical planning. He was described as being blunt and abrasive, but he was very generous with his money, so most people were willing to overlook his less-than-warm-and-cuddly personality.

I was making a second cup of hot chocolate and Hercules was eating a couple of sardine crackers he'd managed to guilt me into getting for him when Marcus called.

"Do you have a list of all the artwork you have at the library—paintings, posters, everything?" he asked.

"I do," I said. The information was on my computer in a spreadsheet.

"I figured you did," he said, and I could hear the smile in his voice. He knew me well.

"I know where a lot of it came from but not everything. I bought probably ninety-five percent of the posters. Most of them are event-specific. Almost all of the paintings were at the library when I arrived. A few of them were donated for that yard sale I told you about. I picked out several that I liked the look of and kept those."

"So was everything being stored in the workroom?"

"Almost everything. Some of the paintings were in several boxes I found in the basement when I first arrived. But I moved everything up into the workroom. I somehow think that watercolor was a donation for the yard sale, but I can't be certain. Susan might remember."

"I'll talk to her," Marcus said. "Could you print off a copy of your list for me? I'll stop by first thing in the morning and pick it up. I can give it a quick look and see if I have any questions."

"I can do that," I said. I smiled even though he couldn't see me. "I can probably be persuaded to make you breakfast as well."

"Umm, I like that idea," he said.

"The persuading or the food?" I teased.

He laughed. "Both. I'll see you in the morning."

I had just finished my own breakfast when Marcus arrived the next morning. Owen and Hercules were still eating. Hercules looked up and meowed a "hello." Owen glanced in Marcus's direction, gave a soft murp and went back to the business of carefully sniffing every bite of food before he ate it.

I kissed Marcus and straightened the collar of his shirt.

"How about a breakfast sandwich on Rebecca's cheese bread with egg, turkey bacon, tomatoes and lettuce?" I asked.

Owen looked up and meowed loudly.

"I wasn't talking to you," I said as I got the eggs from the refrigerator. He flicked his tail at me.

"That sounds good," Marcus said. He got a mug and poured a cup of coffee for himself, then sat at the table. "As soon as I leave here I'm heading to the library. I may be able to release the building sometime this afternoon."

"That would be great," I said. "It would give me a chance to get things cleaned up so we could open on time Saturday morning." I inclined my head toward the table. "That's the list you were looking for."

He picked up the sheet of paper and looked it over. "What does a capital H in brackets after the description mean?" he asked.

"Those are pieces I do have some history for. Remember those paint-by-number birds hanging by the main entrance?"

He nodded.

"Lita's mother painted those. She was an avid birdwatcher. Eventually, I want to add a descriptive note next to each piece of art that I have some background for."

"Maybe you'll get to put a note next to that watercolor that says it was once believed to be a stolen piece of artwork."

I looked over my shoulder at him. "You don't really think that painting is the one that was stolen?" I asked.

He raked a hand back through his hair. "No, I don't. It's just wishful thinking on my part."

"So what happens next?"

"I'm going to call both of those experts Ruby suggested and see if one of them can come to authenticate the painting. I'll also be talking to the detective who worked on the original theft." He took another drink of his coffee. "I want to make sure that Will has no connection at all to that case."

"I don't like to speak ill of the dead, but in my opinion Will liked the easy way out," I said as I sliced a tomato.

"Do you think taking part in an art heist is the easy way out?" Marcus asked. Owen had finished his breakfast and was sitting next to Marcus's chair.

I shook my head. "I don't, but that doesn't mean Will didn't."

Marcus ate his sandwich and I pretended not to see him slip a tiny bit of egg to Owen and to Hercules. He'd gotten much better about not feeding them people food after a stern lecture from Roma.

He folded the list that I'd printed for him and put it in his pocket. Then he kissed me and left, promising he'd call as soon as he knew when I could get back into the library.

I cleaned the kitchen, took some of Rebecca's sourdough bread out of the freezer to thaw and then went down into the basement to start going through boxes, something I'd been putting off for too long.

Marcus and I still hadn't figured out where we were going to live after we were married. I loved my little farmhouse but I didn't own it. It belonged to Everett Henderson, who had originally hired me to supervise the library's renovation. Living in the house was a perk of the job. I liked the neighborhood. There was a sense of belonging that came with knowing everyone on Mountain Road. We were our own little community. Where Marcus lived the lots were larger and there wasn't the same closeness between neighbors.

I liked having Rebecca and Everett on the other side of my backyard and the Justasons next door. I liked being able to walk to work—to pretty much anywhere I wanted to go downtown. I couldn't do that from Marcus's house, but he owned his house. I wasn't sure if that practical reason should carry more weight than my intangible ones.

To my surprise Owen and Hercules got along well with Marcus's little cat, Micah. Like the boys, Micah came from Wisteria Hill. And like them, she wasn't exactly a typical cat. She also had the ability to disappear at will that Owen had. Unlike Owen, she seemed to be a little more circumspect about how and when she used that skill.

I took down a box from the shelves that were next to the laundry sink. Several of the boxes that were stored there held things that had been in the house when I moved in. I'd put off dealing with them way too long. Owen suddenly appeared on top of the dryer. He liked to sit there because it was warm.

"You know, if you had opposable thumbs I'd never have to do laundry again. It's not like you're not down here all the time anyway." He gave me a scornful look and I had the feeling he'd understood every word I'd said.

I undid the flaps of the box. It held dishes that had been left behind in the kitchen cupboards. There were some Spice of Life pieces of CorningWare and a set of colorful Fiestaware nesting bowls. I would have kept the latter if I didn't already have a set. I realized the dishes might be worth something and decided to ask Rebecca about them. I carried the box upstairs and set it in the porch so I wouldn't forget.

Back in the basement I took down two more boxes that were filled with old magazines. They all seemed to be in good shape and they didn't even smell musty after being in the basement for years. I wondered if Maggie or one of the other artists at the co-op would like them. I carried those two boxes upstairs as well, along with some old cans of paint that would need to go to the hazardous waste depot.

I poured another cup of coffee and called Maggie, who said she would love to have the magazines and she would pick them up when she came to get me for the shower on Sunday. I took the cans of paint out to my truck so I wouldn't forget to drop them off at the waste depot. When I came back around the side of the house I spotted Rebecca in her backyard taking a stack of newspapers to her recycling bin. I waved and walked over to join her. I explained about the box of dishes.

"Could I take a look at them?" she asked.

Rebecca was one of those people who always seemed to be smiling. Owen and Hercules adored her. So did pretty much everyone who had ever met her. She was a tiny woman, barely five foot three. She wore her silver hair in a short, layered cut and there was often a gleam of mischief in her blue eyes. Her mother had worked out at Wisteria Hill, which had been Everett's family home. She and Everett had known each other all their lives but had gotten married only a few years ago.

I nodded. "You can take a look at them right now if you want to." We walked back over to my house.

"I think the CorningWare is worth a bit of money," she said, taking two different casserole dishes out of the box. "People collect that kind of thing. Now, I don't know about the bowls. If I didn't have a set myself I'd be tempted to take them. The person you need to talk to is Harrison. Years ago he worked for a while at an auction house."

I frowned. "He did? Why didn't I know that?"

"I have no idea," Rebecca said. "Maybe it never came up."

"So you don't want any of this?" I said, gesturing at the contents of the box.

She smiled and shook her head. "Goodness no. At my age I'm trying to get rid of things."

I smiled back at her. "You are not old and don't try to convince me that you are."

She patted my arm. "Flattery works on me, you know," she

said. She put the casserole dishes back in the cardboard box. "The Reading Buddies kids can have all of this for their yard sale, no matter what it's all worth."

"Thank you," I said. I hesitated. "May I ask you a question? It doesn't have anything to do with any of this."

"Of course," she said.

"Do you think going to prison changed Will Redfern?"

She considered the question for a moment before she answered. "I think going to prison would change anyone."

"But for the better?"

Rebecca smiled. "That's a different question." Her smile faded. "That boy came up hard, you know. His mother was still a teenager when he was born and his father was gone before he started school. Will was carrying around a lot of anger even though he tried to hide it. I remember several years ago he got into some kind of trouble and had to take an anger management class." She shook her head. "No class was going to fix anger that went as deep as that boy's did."

I walked her back to her own yard. "I'll see you Sunday?" I raised one questioning eyebrow.

Rebecca smiled. "I'm always happy to see you," she said, patting my arm, "no matter what day of the week it is."

Clearly, she was in the cone of silence about the shower as well.

Marcus called at lunchtime to tell me I could have my building back.

"Thank you," I said. "Have you learned anything new?"

"No," he said. He hesitated. "This isn't for public consumption yet, but I did find out that Will had an alibi for the time of the original theft of the paintings."

It would have been too easy to find out that he didn't. "Okay, but that doesn't mean he didn't find out about the painting after the fact."

"It doesn't mean he did, either," Marcus said.

I called Mary and Susan, who both said they could come in today to get things back to rights. "I'm at the café," Susan said. "Abigail is here and she says she'll come as well."

I texted Levi, who texted right back to say he would be there after school. It was all hands on deck.

Mary and I arrived at the library at the same time. "The floors will need to be vacuumed at the very least," I said. "And likely mopped as well. I'm guessing the book drop is full. At least it's not sticking for the moment. Oh, and there's a pile of books to be checked in and reshelved that I took out of it yesterday."

"I can start on the books," Mary offered as we walked up the stairs.

"Thank you," I said.

She gave me a long appraising look as we stepped inside the building and I flipped on the lights. "I hate to say I told you so, but I did warn you that Will hadn't changed."

I sighed softly. "I was hoping he had."

"That's because sometimes you are way too nice," Mary said. "I'm not convinced it was a coincidence that my pen disappeared the same afternoon that Will was in this building."

Mary hadn't been able to find her fountain pen and Abigail had misplaced her keys at the end of the day on Tuesday. We'd been moving boxes in the workroom and I suspected that the pen and the keys were going to turn up in one of them. Last time Abigail had lost her keys we'd found them in the book drop.

Mary pointed to the two paintings that flanked the spot where the watercolor had been hanging. Will had tried to pull them off the wall, too. His fingerprints had been on the frames.

"I'm betting that Will tried to get those two paintings down just to cover up the theft of the one painting that was actually worth something. Because I happen to know that neither one of them is worth more than a plugged nickel. Unless someone is a big fan of Daniel Gunnerson."

I laughed because Daniel Gunnerson ran Gunnerson's Funeral Home. Mary and I walked over for a better look at the two paintings.

"They're pretty good," I said. Daniel had painted the doors of two buildings here in town. One was open. One was closed.

"I wouldn't argue with you about that," Mary said, "but I disagree with the sentiment that when one door closes another one opens. When a door closes just open it again. It's a dang door and that's how they work." She turned to look at me. "And if you would like more profound words—Will Redfern was not someone you could or should have trusted." With that she headed for the book drop.

I stared at the bare space where the watercolor had been

hanging. Sadly, it seemed Mary was right. But if Will had come to the library to steal the painting, how did he know it was valuable? How did he know it was here in the first place? Or had he been in the building for some other reason? I had no answers.

chapter 4

We ended up opening late in the afternoon after a lot of phone calls asking when we'd be back to our normal hours.

"I like seeing so many people happy that they can get books," I said to Abigail. We were standing at the circulation desk, where the two of us had just finished clearing a line of people who had been waiting to check out their choices.

"Me too," she said. "I'm also happy that I found my keys and Mary's pen."

Abigail's keys had turned up under the printer stand. Mary's pen was at the bottom of the book drop. I'd missed it but Abigail had spotted it and managed to fish the pen out.

"I think every one of us has dropped something in the book drop at least once," I said. "Levi lost his glasses."

"And half a sandwich," Abigail added with a smile. "Harry wasn't too happy about that."

I smiled back at her. "I'm thinking a new book drop may be my next project. This one jams at least once a month. It's not good for the books."

Abigail grinned and bumped me with her shoulder. "And that's not good because outside of a dog, a book is man's—and woman's—best friend. Inside of a dog, it's too dark to read."

I laughed. Groucho Marx had been right.

Marcus was in my kitchen when I got home. He'd brought Micah with him. She meowed "hello" at me and I bent down to scratch the top of her head. Owen was over by the refrigerator, noisily having a drink. Hercules was sitting forlornly by the table, staring down at his little wind-up mouse.

I picked up the mechanical rodent, wound it and set it at Herc's feet, where it turned in ever-widening circles, much to his enjoyment.

There was bacon in a pan on the stove and sliced tomatoes on the counter.

"Are you making a BLT?" I asked.

Marcus smiled. "I am."

"With lots of mayonnaise?"

He nodded.

I moved closer to him. "And is that BLT for me?"

"It is."

I leaned in and kissed his cheek. "I love you," I said.

His smile got even wider and he nodded. "Yeah, I know," he said.

I sat at the table with my sandwich. It was delicious: Rebecca's sourdough bread, tomatoes from Harry's greenhouse, Burtis Chapman's bacon and enough mayonnaise for two sandwiches.

Owen and Hercules had moved from shadowing Marcus to sitting next to my chair. Micah sat a few feet away, carefully washing her face. I looked down at the boys. "You're not having any bacon. The two of you have been eating way too much people food lately and way too many treats. You know what Roma said."

Owen made grumbling sounds and Hercules got a sour expression on his face. Neither one of them was that fond of Roma. She wasn't just one of my closest friends. Roma was also the person who gave them shots. Micah went on calmly washing her face.

"I found someone to come take a look at that painting," Marcus said. "Her name is Anita Marler. She knows all the stolen artwork well. She was involved in preparations for the exhibit—before the paintings were stolen. She'll be here on Tuesday."

"Have you had any luck finding a connection between Will

and the painting?" I asked. I licked a blob of mayonnaise off my thumb.

Marcus propped an elbow on the table. "None at all. Maybe that stolen painting—assuming that it is the stolen painting—has no connection to Will Redfern at all."

"Because that kind of thing happens all the time."

"Okay, coincidences don't happen very often, but they do happen once in a while."

"So why was Will trying to take that painting if he didn't know it might be worth a lot of money?"

Marcus reached over and snagged a bit of tomato from my plate. "To mess with you. No matter what Will claimed, I agree with Mary. He hadn't really changed. I haven't come up with anything that suggests he really made more than a token effort at being a better person while he was in prison and since he got out. Remember, he only ended up there in the first place because he didn't meet the terms of his community service and probation."

"Fair enough," I said. "But if Will really didn't have any connection to that painting—and I'm not saying I believe that—then who killed him?"

Marcus made a face. "At this point, I don't know, but"—he held up one hand—"his death could be connected to something he was involved in before he went to prison. He could have shortchanged someone on a job. He owed money to some less-than-stellar characters. We could never prove it, but Will may have been involved in that cigarette-smuggling operation we broke up a few years ago. Someone may have been waiting all this time just to get even and they finally saw their chance. There are just too many possibilities."

"No one has a good word for Will," I said. It bothered me that this was how his life had ended. I hadn't heard a word of sadness expressed over the man's death.

"You know as well as I do that he didn't make much of an effort to be a decent person," Marcus said. He leaned back in his chair and stretched his long legs under the table. "Can we talk about something else?"

I nodded. "Tell me how baseball practice is going. You haven't said much." Harry Taylor was coaching a Little League baseball team and he'd recruited—or maybe coerced was more accurate—Marcus to help him.

He smiled. "Turns out it's a lot of fun. The kids are really dedicated and Harry is great with them. He's figured out what each kid's strength is. For instance, Duncan Hollister is a good pitcher. Eight years old and the kid has a slider that will catch you off guard."

"I take it he caught *you* off guard with it."

Marcus laughed and folded one arm behind his head. "More than once. Harry asked me to work with him. He's a great kid and he works really hard."

Duncan and Riley had gone to live with Lita because they had no other close family. Their mother, Bella, was dead, their father was finally in rehab after many years of heavy drinking and near neglect of his kids, and their grandfather was not exactly a good role model for a couple of children.

"After all Duncan and Riley have been through, it makes me happy to hear Duncan has something that makes him happy," I said.

"Me too," Marcus said, leaning in to kiss me.

Out of the corner of my eye I saw his hand snake out to grab a piece of bacon that had fallen out of my sandwich. I snatched it off the plate, held it out of his reach long enough to kiss him and then popped it in my mouth, grinning.

Saturday morning was very busy at the library. Even though we'd been closed for less than two full days it seemed we'd been missed. I was happy to see so many people borrowing books and movies and looking through our new seed collection and spending very little time trying to figure out where Will Redfern's body had been found. The news about Will had gotten around town pretty quickly, just as I'd known it would, and the police had had to release a statement confirming that he had died in the building.

We had taken down the two remaining paintings from the section of wall where the watercolor had been hanging and replaced them with a poster of Paddington Bear and a poster of the cover of Todd Parr's *It's Okay to Be Different.* The bright colors of the latter made me smile.

When the building closed at lunchtime I drove out to see Harrison Taylor. I had called him about the dishes from the basement and he'd said he would be happy to take a look at them for me.

I found the old man and his dog, Boris, waiting on the back patio of his little house. I hugged both of them. The first time I'd seen Harrison Taylor I'd thought Santa Claus was sitting in my backyard. He had a head full of white hair and a snowy white beard, as well as a twinkle in his blue eyes.

His son had inherited Harrison's kind heart and work ethic. Unfortunately he hadn't gotten the hair gene.

Harry had the barbeque going. "How about a burger and some broccoli slaw?" the younger Taylor asked with a smile. Harrison's house was on Harry's property. That meant Harry could keep an eye on his father but they both had their privacy and the dog could travel back and forth between the two houses.

"Thank you. That sounds wonderful," I said. "We were so busy I didn't get a break all morning."

I set the cardboard box down at the old man's feet and he opened the top flaps. Boris poked his nose in to take a look as well.

"Move out of the way, boy," Harrison said.

Boris lifted his head and looked at the old man but he stayed where he was. I patted the side of my leg. "C'mon over here," I said to the dog.

He turned from the box and came to sit beside me, setting

his head in my lap and looking up at me with his chocolate brown eyes.

"Oh, you he listens to you," Harrison grumbled. I could see a hint of a smile pulling at the corners of his mouth so I knew he wasn't really annoyed.

"Well, Kathleen's a lot prettier than you are," Harry said. "Dog's not stupid."

"Can't argue with that," Harrison replied. He reached into the box and pulled out the set of Fiestaware bowls, turning each one over to check the markings on the bottom. Finally he looked over at me. "These are old and they're in very good shape," he said. "They're worth some money. Forty, maybe fifty dollars each."

Harrison made quick work of checking the CorningWare casserole dishes, pointing out which pieces were vintage and would be worth more to a collector. "Rebecca said she's giving all of this to the kids for their yard sale?" he asked.

I nodded. "They're trying to raise enough money to buy books for a first-grade classroom in an inner-city school." Harry set a cup of coffee in front of me, and I mouthed a thank-you. "It was all the kids' idea," I continued as I added cream and sugar to my cup, stirred and took a sip. "I'm so proud of them. They even came up with the plan to have a yard sale by themselves."

"Tell Ruby to call me before the sale and I'll help them with pricing," Harrison said. "And I'll see if we have anything around here to contribute."

I smiled at him. "Thank you," I said. "I will."

"Why do I think it'll end up being my stuff that gets contributed, not yours?" Harry asked.

"Darned if I know," his father said.

Harry brought my food to the table then. The burger was done just the way I liked it, with onions and a slice of cheddar cheese. I added a little ketchup and took a bite. "Oh, that's good," I said to Harry.

"Thank you," he said. He got himself a cup of coffee and joined us at the table. "Marcus having any luck figuring out what happened to Will Redfern?" he asked.

"Not yet," I said, picking up my fork to try the broccoli slaw. It was as good as my burger. "You know the kind of people that Will associated with. It's not going to be easy."

"That wasn't all the boy's fault," Harrison said. Harry gave his head an almost imperceptible shake. The old man looked across the table at his son. "What's that look for? I'm not excusing anything he did. I'm just trying to give Kathleen some context."

"He broke her wrist, Dad," Harry said. "I think Kathleen has all the context she needs when it comes to Will Redfern."

Boris was lying at my feet. He lifted his head at the sound of the men's voices. I reached down and patted his head, and he stretched out again. "It's okay," I said to Harry. I looked over at his father. "I'm listening. Go ahead." This was the first time anyone other than Rebecca had given any grace to Will and I wanted to hear what the old man had to say.

"Will's mother was sixteen years old when he was born. She had four kids by the time she was twenty-one, with no family around, and a husband who took off before the fourth one was even born. It took all of her time and effort to put food in their bellies and a roof over their head. Will needed more than she had to give him."

He rubbed his gnarled fingers together. "Yes, that boy always took the easy way out, but that's because he had no one to teach him anything else, teaching him right from wrong. His father died when Will was a teenager, not that he was around anyway. No one knows where his mother ended up. She's likely dead as well now. Any one of us could have turned out the same way in those same circumstances. I'm not asking you to cut Will any slack given what he did to you, and I'm not making any excuses for him. I just think you ought to know how he got to where he ended up."

I thought about my own parents, especially my mother, who loved all three of us fiercely but also insisted on hard work and helping others. And I thought about Lonnie Hollister, who was trying to do right by his children at last but was struggling to get there. I reached across the table and laid my hand over Harrison's for a moment. "Thanks for telling me," I said.

Harry got to his feet. He indicated my cup. "How about a refill?"

"Please," I said.

He picked up my mug and gave his father's shoulder a quick squeeze as he moved around the table.

I stayed for another half an hour talking to Harrison about his daughter, Elizabeth, who was headed to medical school and his other son Larry's stepdaughter, Emmy, who had become another much-loved granddaughter for Harrison. "You better save me a dance at the wedding," he teased. "I've been practicing."

"You better wear your dancing shoes," I retorted.

The old man laughed. "You just concentrate on keepin' up with me."

Harry and Boris walked me out to the truck when I left. "Kathleen, be careful," Harry said. "Everything the old man said about Will is true. He did get screwed over by life. But he also made a lot of bad choices and one of those bad choices may have gotten him killed. Just keep an eye out for a while."

"I will," I said.

Marcus and I decided to have supper at Fern's Diner before we headed to the airport to pick up his sister, Hannah, who was flying in from New York for the shower. She was in rehearsals for a new play so she would be heading back right after, but we were both happy to have even a little time with her. She was a talented actor, more and more in demand, and we hadn't seen her since New Year's.

Over meatloaf, mashed potatoes and lots (and lots) of gravy I told Marcus what Harrison had said.

"He's not wrong, you know. Will came up hard. No one really had any time for him."

"I know he had some criminal connections. Do you think any of those people could have killed him?"

Marcus set down his fork and reached for his glass. "I told you we always felt he was involved in that cigarette-smuggling case."

"I remember," I said.

"More than one of those people wouldn't have hesitated to do something to Will but they all have alibis."

"Solid ones?" I asked

"Solid as a jail cell," he said.

chapter 5

Hannah's plane was right on time. Marcus spotted her first in the crowd of people walking toward us. She grinned and waved when she caught sight of us. I was touched that Hannah had flown halfway across the country for basically twenty-four hours just to celebrate the fact that I was marrying her brother and even happier now that I saw how happy Marcus was to see her. His smile stretched from ear to ear as he threw his arms around her.

"I'm so glad to be here," Hannah said when it was my turn to hug her. She narrowed her blue eyes. "And don't you dare say I didn't have to come all this way just for you. I wouldn't have missed this for anything." She turned to smile at her brother. "And I get to spend a bit of time with this guy, too."

Hannah told us all about the play she was rehearsing for as we drove back to Mayville Heights. It was a family drama and Hannah had a major role as the oldest child. She was a gifted actor and I was hoping this would be her big break.

I stayed at Marcus's place for about an hour, catching up with Hannah and answering all her questions abut the wedding. Then I headed home to give the two of them some brother and sister time since she'd be leaving right after the shower on Sunday.

"You'll be back for breakfast, right?" Hannah asked as I pulled on my hoodie. "I'm cooking. Omelets with cheese and cornmeal scones."

"I'll be here," I said. Hannah was a terrific cook. She'd been experimenting in the kitchen since she was a kid. She was both exacting and creative.

Marcus walked me out to the truck, which I'd left at his place when we'd headed down to Fern's for supper. He kissed me and I laid my head against his chest for a moment. "Love you," I said.

"Lucky me," he replied.

I could hear the strong, steady thump, thump, thump of his heartbeat. "No," I said. "Lucky me."

Marcus had the coffee waiting when I got to his house on Sunday morning. I sat at the table with Micah on my lap and talked to Hannah while she worked. She made fluffy omelets and cheesy scones, swatting her brother with an oven mitt when he tried to peek at the latter in the oven. After a second cup of coffee we left Marcus with the dishes and headed out to Ella King's so Hannah could try on her bridesmaid dress. Ella was a gifted seamstress. She was making all four bridesmaid dresses and my wedding dress.

My breath caught in my throat when Hannah came out in her dress. It had a round neckline, delicate flutter sleeves and a long, flowing skirt in a pale blue-green color Ella called seafoam. "You look so beautiful," I said.

"I feel beautiful in this dress," Hannah said. She smiled at Ella. "You've done a wonderful job."

"You have," I agreed.

"Thank you," Ella said. "It fits perfectly. All I need to do is pin the hem."

Once Ella was satisfied with the length of the dress, Hannah and I drove back to Marcus's house. I was heading home to change for the party.

"I'll see you later," Hannah said as she got out of the truck.

"I don't even know where we're going," I said.

She nodded. "I know."

"You know that I *don't* know, or you know where the party is?" I asked.

She grinned. "Both." Then she gave me a little wave and disappeared around the side of the house.

I wondered how Maggie and Roma had managed to keep every detail of the shower a secret from me. I had no idea where we were going or what we were doing. Since I was a bit of a control freak, it was driving me crazy.

Maggie picked me up just before one. She had said that Owen would help me choose what to wear and it turned out she wasn't wrong. He'd stood in front of the closet door and meowed loudly, wrinkling his whiskers at my first four choices. Finally I (we) settled on a blue dress with short sleeves and a full skirt. We were just choosing my shoes when Marcus's mom called.

"I'm sorry I'm not there," she said. Celeste was a wildlife biologist, involved in a long-term study of polar bears in Norway.

"I understand," I said. "You'll be here for the wedding and that's what I care about."

We talked for a couple of minutes and then said good-bye. Owen had taken the opportunity to nudge the pair of shoes he thought I should wear out of the closet.

I slipped my feet into them. They went with the dress and they were comfortable. "Okay, you were right about the shoes, too," I said. "Don't let that go to your head."

He gave me a decidedly smug look. The only thing Owen liked more than being right was me acknowledging it.

"Oh, I like the dress," Maggie said when she stepped into the kitchen a short time later. She was wearing a flowy yellow jumpsuit. She smiled down at Owen. "Good choice."

He cocked his head to one side and gave her his usual adoring look.

Maggie smiled back at him. "Your mother's plane landed about half an hour ago," she said to me. "But you probably already know that."

I nodded. "She called me from the airport." Mom was coming from Los Angeles, where she was halfway through her latest stint on the popular soap *The Wild and the Wonderful*. She was supposed to arrive on Saturday, but bad weather between California and Minnesota had delayed her flight twice. She had to be on set early Monday morning but at least I'd have a few hours with her.

We put the boxes of magazines I'd saved for Maggie in the back of her bug. Then we pulled out of the driveway and turned right up the hill.

"We're going out to Roma's," I said.

"Yes, we are," Maggie said, keeping her eyes on the road.

"So who's going to be there?" I asked.

"You'll see soon enough."

"At least tell me what we're going to be doing."

Her gaze flicked over to me for a moment. "You'll see that soon enough, too," she said.

"Why so much secrecy?" I said, twisting my engagement ring around my finger.

"Why so many nosy questions?" she retorted.

"I'm just curious about what's going to happen."

Maggie laughed. "You know I love you, but you are a con-trol freak, Kathleen. Your job today is just to enjoy yourself."

"I already am," I said. "Thank you. Thank you for every-thing. For today. For playing matchmaker. For being such an incredible friend."

Maggie glanced over at me again. "I'm so happy we're friends," she said. "And I'm so happy you and Marcus are get-ting your happily ever after."

We turned up Roma's driveway and I remembered the first time I saw the old Henderson estate, back when Everett still owned Wisteria Hill. So many good things had come into my life because of this place.

I had sold my car when I'd moved to Minnesota and I'd spent the first couple of weeks in Mayville Heights exploring the town and surrounding area. I'd walked for miles at a time. I'd been trying to get over a broken heart and the walking had helped.

Owen and Hercules had been two tiny balls of fur that had followed me down the driveway at Wisteria Hill. At that time it was nothing more than a couple of muddy ruts in the ground. I'd picked up the kittens and carried them back to the empty farmhouse. There was no sign of their mother in the over-grown bushes and weeds.

Halfway down the driveway for a second time I'd looked back to see the two tiny cats coming behind me again, picking their way over the wet ground and stopping every so often to shake a paw. I knew I couldn't leave them behind. Now I couldn't imagine life without them, although most of the time they acted more like roommates than pets.

I got out of the car and looked over at the old carriage house, which was where the wedding was going to take place. I had no idea what it looked like inside at the moment. That was a more closely guarded secret than Maggie and Roma's plans for my shower, but Roma's husband, Eddie, was in charge of the renovations and I had faith that whatever he did to the old building would look wonderful. I just wanted to marry Marcus.

The carriage house did have a lot of sentimental meaning for me, though. For a long time it had been the home of the feral cat colony that lived out at Wisteria Hill. Roma had organized a group of volunteers to feed and check on the cats, who were very skittish, for the most part, around people. She had paired Marcus and me, and we had slowly gotten to know each other better as we worked together.

Maggie put a hand on my shoulder. "Eddie said you can't look yet, and if you try I'm supposed to check you into the boards." Eddie was a former NHL player. She held up one foot. "Please don't make me do that, because I'm not wearing the right kind of shoes for body-checking anyone."

I laughed and headed toward the side door to the farmhouse, where Roma was waiting. She pulled me into a hug. "I'm so glad to see you," she said. "I've been waiting for this moment since the day I paired you and Marcus for cat duty."

"I was just remembering that," I said. "Marcus and I spent a lot of time out here together."

"That's why I did it," Roma said. "Now come inside. It's time to celebrate."

All of my favorite people were standing in Roma's dining room. Hannah, of course. Rebecca. Lita. Abigail. Mary and Susan. Taylor and Ella. Ruby. Georgia. Riley. I hugged everyone and had to blink back tears more than once. Mom had texted that she and Brady Chapman, Maggie's . . . guy, I still didn't know what else to call him . . . who had picked Mom up, were less than half an hour away. I knew better than to ask if they'd obeyed the posted speed limits. The only person we were missing, aside from Marcus's mother, was my sister, Sarah, who was working on another documentary.

"There's a package in the living room that won't keep," Roma said. "You need to open it now."

The mysterious package that they had been talking about. I looked at Maggie. "What did you do?" I asked.

"*We* didn't do anything," she said.

I stepped into the living room wondering just what I was going to find. Sarah was standing in the middle of the room. She grinned and held out both hands. "Surprise!"

For a moment I just stood there, rooted to the floor in shock. Then I threw my arms around her. "I don't understand," I said. "How did you get here? I thought you were on the road with the Hypochondriacs, working on your documentary."

Sarah was a makeup artist and a filmmaker. This was the second behind-the-scenes film about an up-and-coming band she'd worked on.

"I was. I mean I am," she said, pulling back to grin at me. She'd added a second earring to her left earlobe and her hair was cut to a just-below-chin-length bob. "I grabbed a ride with another band as far as Minneapolis. I got in in the middle of the night. Eddie picked me up this morning. I couldn't let Mom be the only one to represent our family. Besides, how often does a person get married?"

"Twice. Three times, tops," a voice said behind me.

I turned around to find Mom standing there. I gave a squeal of happiness and pulled her into a hug. "I can't believe both of you made it," I said, reaching out one hand to pull Sarah closer. I turned to look at Roma and Maggie, who were smiling and looking very pleased with themselves. I held out a hand to each of them. "Best day ever," I said, stealing Roma's favorite expression.

We ate first. Roma's long dining room table had been replaced with several smaller round ones set with white tablecloths, blue and green flowered napkins and small vases filled with white tulips that I guessed came from Burtis Chapman's greenhouse. I saw three chairs from Rebecca's kitchen and three more from Lita's.

Taylor King, Riley and Susan served us small salads first and then Maggie's pizza.

"How did you manage to do this and everything else?" I asked.

Maggie smiled. She couldn't seem to stop smiling. "Easy. I shared my pizza recipe with Eddie," she said.

"This is perfect," I said, getting up to hug her. I couldn't seem to stop hugging people.

Georgia had made a cupcake tower with four different kinds of cupcakes for dessert and there was tea and coffee. "I think I have a solution to your wedding cake dilemma," she said when I went to her table to thank her. I still hadn't decided what kind of cake I liked best. And Marcus wasn't any better at choosing than I was.

Georgia held up three fingers. "Three layers. Three different flavors."

I nodded. "Yes. I like that."

She tipped her head to one side and studied my face. "You *can* narrow it down to three kinds of cake, can't you?"

"Yes," I said. "Probably. Maybe."

She laughed. "I'll call you in a couple of days."

I slipped out to the kitchen to thank Eddie.

He was at the sink wearing a denim apron with the words **Hot Stuff** on the front.

"I was glad to do it," he said when I thanked him for the pizza. "The fact that I got Maggie's sauce recipe is just a happy bonus."

Roma and Maggie had decided this was going to be a cooking shower. Each guest had brought a small kitchen gift and was sharing a favorite recipe with me.

Rebecca gave me a reproduction 1960s turquoise metal breadbox and the recipe for her honey sunny bread. "It doesn't mean I won't still show up at your back door with a loaf," she said.

"You better," I said.

Roma shared Eddie's recipe for chili and gave me a pepper mill. Susan gave me her husband Eric's chocolate pudding recipe and a set of four vintage blue bubble glass bowls. They matched the bubble glass plates I already had.

Mom and Sarah's gift was the china gravy boat that had belonged to our dad's mom, along with a packet of gravy mix. "Because everyone knows Kathleen is the only decent cook in our family," Sarah said.

I blew a kiss to both of them.

Hannah shared their family's ginger cookie recipe and a teddy bear police officer cookie jar. "I thought it looked like my big brother," she said with a grin.

Lita gave me her coffee cake recipe and a French press to make the coffee to go with the cake.

From Georgia I received her buttercream frosting recipe and a piping bag with tips.

Peggy's gift was Harrison's meatloaf recipe and a vintage hand crank meat grinder.

Ruby gave me her grandmother's recipe for apple butter and two beautiful hand-carved wooden spoons.

Taylor and Ella's gift was their family recipe for marmalade and half a dozen glass canning jars, and Ella promised she'd come help me make it the first time.

SOFIE KELLY

"I'm holding you to that," I said.

Riley gave me a cake pan and her mother's apple cake recipe in Bella's handwriting. I hugged her tightly, my chest heavy with emotion.

"Promise you'll come make it with me," I said.

She nodded.

Mary was the last person to stand up. Smiling, she handed me a vegetable peeler. "I know you were expecting my cinnamon roll recipe," she said.

I'd been trying to duplicate Mary's cinnamon roll recipe for years. I'd come close but never quite gotten it. And I'd never been able to convince her to share the ingredients.

She held out a folded sheet of paper. I opened it and scanned the recipe. The secret ingredient was . . . potatoes? I looked at Mary. "Seriously?"

"Yes."

I shook my head. "I never would have figure that out," I said.

She smiled. "Be happy," she said. "You've earned it."

After all the gifts had been opened I got to spend a few minutes with Riley. She wore a short black skirt with a blue-and-black short-sleeved shirt and her black Doc Martens. "I'm so glad you came," I said.

"Yeah, me too," she said. "I like Eddie. He said he'll teach me how to cook."

"He's a very good cook. You should take him up on that offer."

"Did you mean it about making the cake together?" she asked.

"Absolutely," I said. "We'll probably have a couple of furry supervisors, though." I hated the fact that the adults in her life had been so unreliable she didn't take me at my word.

"That's okay," she said with a shrug. "I'm starting to think I'm more of a cat person than a dog person. I mean I like dogs and all, but Roma says I have a way with cats."

Roma had told me the same thing. "She'd make a wonderful vet," she'd said.

"Cats are very good judges of character," I said.

Riley shrugged. "Yeah, well I don't know about that." She folded her arms over her chest. "You, um, you could thank Marcus for me when you see him for all the time he's spent working with Duncan on his pitching. The squirt loves baseball, but Lonnie was never sober enough to teach him anything and the old man never gave a crap about anyone besides himself."

Riley always called her father by his given name, her reasoning being that he never acted like a dad, so why should she call him that? And she never referred to her grandfather by any other name besides "the old man" or "he." When Harry called his father "the old man" I could hear the love in the words. When Riley used the words for Gerald all I could hear was contempt.

I nodded. "I'll tell him."

She looked down at the floor for a moment. "We saw Lonnie yesterday," she said.

"How is he?" I asked.

"He's still not drinking. He's not the way he used to be, either."

I frowned. "What do you mean?"

"He used to make so many excuses, you know, for all the ways he sucked at being a father. He doesn't do that anymore. He's still . . . he's still not a very good dad but at least he admits it now." She rubbed her shoulder with one hand. "Lita says he didn't have a very good role model. Boy is that the truth. *He* wants to spend time with us, you know."

"Gerald?" I said. Since when was he interested in his grandchildren?

Riley nodded. "Yeah. I told him to forget it. Duncan's afraid of him. I'm not making him go out to the farm and I'm not going anywhere near that place. Lita told him no. He was pissed but he left." Her eyes darkened.

As Mary would say, I didn't trust Gerald Hollister as far as I could throw him. "If he gives you any trouble about anything, you call me," I said. "I mean it."

She nodded. "Okay. I will."

"This is supposed to be my day," I said, holding out both of my hands. "So could I maybe have a hug?"

Riley gave an exaggerated sigh. "Yes, you can have a hug." She couldn't hold back her smile. I wrapped my arms around her and hoped that there were enough people who loved her that she wouldn't end up like Will.

Sarah and Hannah had to leave early. Brady was taking them to the airport.

I hugged them both. "Thank you for doing all of this for me," I said. "It wouldn't have been the same without either one of you."

"Marcus is happier than I've ever seen him," Hannah said. "And that's because of you."

Sarah smiled. "Even when you were a pain in the ass you were the best big sister anyone could have," she said.

I couldn't speak.

Sarah linked an arm with Hannah. "We love you," she said.

"And we'll be back for the wedding," Hannah added. And then they were gone.

Rebecca put an arm around my shoulders. "You look a little overwhelmed."

I nodded. "I am. Sarah and Hannah and everyone else went to so much trouble for me."

"We all love you," she said. She reached up and patted my cheek. "It wasn't any trouble."

People began to leave after that. Soon only Roma, Maggie, Mom and I were left. Eddie was in the kitchen and had shooed us out when we'd offered to help.

"Would you like a peek inside the carriage house?" Roma asked.

"Yes, I would," I said. I glanced over at Maggie. She'd taken off her heels and was wearing a pair of flip-flops belonging to Roma that were at least one size too small. "But I don't want to get checked into the boards by Maggie."

Maggie laughed. "It's okay. Eddie let me off the hook before he started the dishes."

We walked across the yard and Roma let us inside the carriage house. I reached for Mom's hand.

I don't know what I was expecting to see but it was nothing like what was waiting inside.

I felt my breath catch in my throat. The space had been transformed.

The walls and the ceiling had been painted a soft cream color. So had the floor. The beams overhead were all stained a deep shade of gray. Three evenly spaced sphere-shaped chandeliers were suspended from the ceiling so the entire space glowed with light. There were new windows flanking and up above the new door and a bank of more windows at the far end of the huge room.

I pressed my fist against my mouth. I couldn't speak. Maggie laid her head against mine and put one hand on my shoulder.

"Is it all right?" Roma asked.

Did I hear a little uncertainty in her voice? I nodded. "It's absolutely perfect," I said when I could finally get words out. "How did Eddie get all of this done? He must have worked day and night."

"He had a lot of help," Roma said. "Brady. Larry and Harry. Keith King. Oren. Burtis. Even your future husband. Eric sent food up and Harrison helped Eddie come up with the plans and work out all the details."

"It's absolutely beautiful," Mom said. She gave my hand a squeeze, then let go and turned in a slow circle, taking in every detail of the space.

Roma pointed out where the tables would be set up along with strings of lights and battery-powered candles.

I was overwhelmed. "I don't know how to thank you," I said. "Not just for this." I gestured with one hand. "For everything you've done."

"That's easy," Roma said. "Be happy. There aren't nearly as many chances to do that as you might think so grab every one of them."

We put all my gifts in the back of Maggie's car and she and Mom and I headed back to town. We drove a little way in silence.

"It was a good day," Maggie finally said.

"It was," I agreed. I looked over at her. She had the little frown on her forehead she always got when she drove. "One of the best things about coming to Mayville Heights was meeting you and Roma," I said.

Maggie glanced over at me. "For us, too."

"I can't believe how much my life has changed."

"Maybe it just all worked out the way it was supposed to," Mom said from the backseat.

I turned to smile at her. "Maybe it did."

Owen and Hercules were waiting in the kitchen for us. Mom bent down to talk to both of them.

Finally she stood up and wrapped me in a hug. "It's so good to be here," she said. "I wish I could stay longer."

"Me too," I said. "But I'll take a little of you over none of you at all."

I was the reason my mother was on *The Wild and the Wonderful* at the moment. She was crazy popular with the fans of the long-running soap and the producers would happily have signed her to a long-term contract but she wasn't interested. Her first love was the stage. However, she was willing to drop in for short visits. The current one had come about when my mother—and the rest of the family—had hitched a ride on the production company's plane to come for a visit. In return she'd agreed to six weeks on the set. She was at the halfway point. By the time her episodes aired she'd be back in Boston.

"I'm just going to go take off this makeup and then I want to hear all about what's happening at the library," Mom said.

I nodded. "Go ahead. You know where everything is."

Mom headed upstairs and I looked down to see that Owen and Hercules were staring at the small box of cupcakes I had set on the table. "Not a chance," I told them, but I gave each of them a bite of chicken and a hug. Hercules gave his brother a bewildered look and Owen seemed to shrug.

I had decided something on the drive home. "I am incredibly blessed," I told the two of them. "If Will Redfern had had even a few people in his life like I have, there's no way he would have done all the things he'd done. It wasn't fair. So I'm going to even things out."

The boys exchanged a look.

"We're going to find out who killed him," I said.

chapter 6

Mom and I had supper. She shared stories from the set and I brought her up-to-date on what had been happening in Mayville Heights. Before we knew it Marcus arrived for the drive back to Minneapolis.

I gave her one last hug before she went through security at the airport. "I love you, Katydid," she said.

"I love you, too," I said.

Mom kissed Marcus on the cheek. "Take good care of my girl," she told him.

He smiled. "Always."

She blew me a kiss and she was gone. I leaned against Marcus's chest and he wrapped his arms around me. I sighed softly.

I already missed Mom and she was barely out of sight, but I'd meant what I had told Owen and Hercules. I was going to figure out who was responsible for Will Redfern's death.

I needed to know more about the man, I decided. I sat at the table with my breakfast Monday morning, trying to figure out whom I could talk to about Will. His father was dead and no one knew if his mother was alive. I remembered Harrison saying she was likely dead as well. Mary had mentioned that Will's youngest sister lived somewhere in Michigan, but they hadn't seen or spoken to each other in years. I had no idea how to find her and I didn't see how she'd be able to tell me much about her brother.

"Do you think Will had any friends?" I said to Hercules. He looked up from his breakfast and wrinkled his nose. He didn't seem to know, either.

I settled for making a list of the names of the men who had worked with Will on the library renovation. At least it was somewhere to start. Then I checked Will's obituary online, but there were no details about his family or friends. It was very sparse, which left me feeling a little sad. I remembered that Will had been interested in Ingrid, the librarian I had replaced. I made a mental note to ask Abigail or Mary if they knew anything about her.

Hercules had finished eating and was sitting at my feet,

washing his tail. "I wonder if Marcus would tell me the name of Will's prison cellmate," I said.

The cat looked at me like I was crazy.

"He might," I said.

"Mrrr," he said. I had the feeling he would have rolled his eyes if he could.

I decided the best approach was a multipart one. I'd try to find the men who had worked with Will at the library. Since they knew who I was, there was at least a chance they would talk to me. And I'd see what I could learn about the theft of Robert Hamilton's paintings and who the main suspects were. I couldn't shake the feeling that somehow Will was connected to that robbery. I also decided that I would ask Mary more about Will's visit to the library.

I spent the next half hour using the library's newspaper database to find several articles about the Hamilton art theft. Law enforcement had believed the robbery was an inside job because it was so well planned and executed so quickly, but all the major players had alibis. In the end I made a list of people whose names seemed to come up over and over, including the art historian, the researcher and two of the guards at Hamilton's house. I also learned that Hamilton's wife at the time was briefly a person of interest because the two of them were in the middle of an acrimonious divorce.

I took the box of dishes that Harrison had gone through down to the library to store in the basement for the kids' yard sale. At the shower Ruby had said she would try to stop in with a few more boxes to be stored. She showed up just after ten o'clock with a box of tools—some vintage, some almost new—that Burtis Chapman had donated.

"He's a big softie," I said to Ruby.

She nodded. "He claimed he just wanted everything out of his shop, but you know he's the first to step up for anything that involves kids."

She also had a big box of baby clothes. "Oh, those should sell quickly," I said.

She smiled. "That's what I'm hoping." We put the boxes in the basement and came back upstairs.

Ruby gestured to the two posters that had replaced the paintings. "I like those."

"I wanted to take the focus away from what happened to Will," I said. "And I didn't want people speculating about the other two paintings hanging there."

"I still can't figure out how that watercolor ended up here of all places," she said. "It's driving me crazy. I never thought of Will Redfern as someone with an interest in art. Do you think he knew what he was stealing?"

"I don't know. It seems like an awfully big coincidence that he seemed to be trying to take the one piece of artwork in the building that may be worth something."

"How many other paintings do you have?" Ruby asked, looking around.

"There are all the ones you can see hanging in various places on this floor and there's close to a dozen up in the workroom, believe it or not."

"Would you mind if I look at the ones upstairs?" Ruby asked. "I'm not trying to give the impression I think the building is a refuge for stolen art." Her gaze slipped away from mine.

"But," I said.

Ruby slid the half-dozen bracelets she was wearing up and down her right arm. Her eyes met mine again. "First of all, this is nothing more than gossip and speculation, but there have always been rumors that there might have been some artwork stolen from Robert Hamilton that *wasn't* on the insurance list."

"Do you mean something that he didn't have provenance for?" I asked. Provenance was the history of a piece of art, receipts and other documents. Among other things, provenance was important for proving the legitimacy of a piece of artwork.

She nodded. "There are always rumors in a situation like that. Mr. Hamilton has a reputation for being ruthless when he goes after something, whether it's in business or in his personal life. People have always speculated that he has another art collection that's for his eyes only and that none of those pieces have been acquired legally."

"So if the painting that was here is from what we'll call

Hamilton's public collection, then maybe there's also something here from his private collection."

She gave me a sheepish look. "I know how bizarre that sounds."

"Ruby, there's a good possibility that a valuable—and stolen—painting has been sitting in a box here in the library for more than five years," I said. "What you're suggesting doesn't sound that outrageous. Let's go take a look." What I didn't say was that I was curious, too.

The paintings were in two boxes on a shelf in the workroom. Ruby looked at each one. She pointed out three where she recognized the signature—they weren't worth anything—and a fourth that she knew that Daniel Gunnerson had painted. It was a window instead of his usual doors.

"I don't see anything that looks significant," she said after she'd checked out the contents of both boxes, "but I'm no expert. It *might* be worth talking to someone with more knowledge than I have. Isn't Anita Marler coming soon to look at that painting that Will tried to steal?"

I nodded. "This week, unless something has changed."

"Maybe she'd take a look at these paintings as well."

"What can you tell me about her?" I asked. Anita Marler was on my list of people to check out. She had been hired to check the provenance—the credentials, in essence—for Robert Hamilton's artwork. And for a while she'd been a suspect in the robbery.

"Not very much," Ruby said. "I've never met her, but I keep

in touch with one of my professors and he's the one who suggested contacting her. Anita was cleared pretty quickly of having anything to do with the Hamilton theft. She had a rock-solid alibi. He says she has an excellent eye for detail and color and a superb memory. She knows all of those paintings well. Maybe she'll have some idea of how that watercolor ended up here."

Marcus called at lunchtime. "Anita Marler will be in town tomorrow," he said. "I'd like her to look at the other paintings you have over there," he said. "Could I bring her by about eleven o'clock?"

"Ruby suggested the same thing," I said. "And yes, eleven o'clock works fine for me. Do you have time for a quick question?"

"Sure," he said. "What is it?"

"I'd like to know more about Will's cellmate. What's his name, for instance?"

"Why?" There was a note of caution in his voice, apparent even just in that one word.

"Because Will's dead. I want to know who killed him."

"That's my job," Marcus said. "Not yours."

I felt a tiny jab of irritation. "I know," I said. "But this is my library. And I'm the one who found Will's body."

"Which doesn't mean you have any obligation to him." He paused. "Will hurt you. Why do you care about finding his killer?"

"Because nobody else seems to care," I said.

"I care," Marcus said.

I took a deep breath and let it out slowly before I answered. "I know that. But it's your job to figure out who killed Will. His death doesn't seem to matter to a single person in town. His obituary is just one paragraph. I think it's sad that his life came to that. Who is it going to hurt if I ask a few questions?"

The silence stretched between us before he finally spoke. "I'm sorry, I can't give you his cellmate's name but I can tell you that he doesn't seem to have any criminal connections. The man embezzled money from a kids' sports program. He's a guy whose taste for the finer things in life exceeds his work ethic."

"So you think he's a dead end."

I heard his chair squeak, which told me he was at his desk. "Yeah, I do. The guy got out a month before Will did and he's kept his nose clean so far. He has no connection whatsoever to the Hamilton robbery and no connection to the art world. The guy has no possible connection to any of this. You're not missing anything."

"Is it possible Will did any work for Robert Hamilton at some point?" I asked.

"I had the same idea but so far I can't find a single connection between the two of them. Right now I'm leaning toward something or someone else from Will's past catching up with him."

"So you're saying him trying to take a painting that was

likely stolen was just a coincidence," I said. "I thought you didn't believe in coincidences."

Marcus laughed. "In general, I don't, but once you eliminate the impossible, whatever remains, no matter how coincidental, must be the truth."

It was my turn to laugh. "That's not exactly what Sir Arthur Conan Doyle wrote."

"It's the essence of what he wrote." I could hear voices in the background. "I have to go," he said. "I'll see you for supper. Have a good day."

Abigail had an elementary class tour after lunch. As usual she was great with the kids. The fact that she didn't talk down to them was part of what made her such a good writer for young people.

Duncan's class was part of the group. He smiled and gave me a shy wave. I waved back. At the end of the tour the two classes gathered by the circulation desk and I was surrounded by kids with questions about everything from how did I pick out the books to which ones would I save in a fire to did I know any real authors who weren't dead. The last question was always my favorite because I got to point at Abigail and hold up a couple of her books.

As most of the kids crowded around her calling out questions, Duncan came over to me. "Did you like the tour?" I asked.

He shrugged. "It was okay, but I pretty much knew everything already."

"That's because you're in Reading Buddies," I said.

"I kind of knew a bunch of stuff before that because Riley knows everything about the library," he said.

I nodded. "You're right. I think Riley knows almost as much as I do."

He nodded thoughtfully. "Maybe when you get really old she could be the boss of the library."

"I think she'd be very good at it," I said. "What do you think?"

"I think she'd be good at it, too," he said, "but I think Riley should take care of animals like Dr. Davidson does because whenever she comes back from Dr. Davidson's clinic she's in a good mood. Sometimes she even sings, really quiet, if she thinks no one can hear her."

I leaned closer to him. "I'll tell you a secret. Sometimes when I'm here in the library by myself I sing. Sometimes I even dance."

Duncan smiled. "I won't tell. I bet you're a good dancer."

I made a face and he laughed. "What do you want to be when you're grown up?" I asked.

He scuffed the floor with the toe of his black sneakers. "I want to be a baseball player."

"I heard that you're a pretty good pitcher."

He squared his shoulders and stood up a little straighter. "Marcus says I am and I've been practicing a lot. Riley says pitching is just math, but she thinks everything is math." He shifted from one foot to the other. "Would you come to see my first game? It's on Saturday."

I nodded. "I would love to come to your game."

His smile returned. "Did you play baseball when you were my age?" he asked.

"I did," I said. "But I wasn't very good at it. I could hit the ball, but I was awful at throwing it. I'm still not that good at throwing sometimes. The ball doesn't always go where I want it to."

A frown creased Duncan's forehead. "It could be your feet."

I put one hand on my hip. "Wait a minute, I thought I was supposed to throw with my hands."

That made him laugh again. Behind us the teachers were rounding up the kids. He glanced over his shoulder. "I have to go but I'll show you what I mean when you come to my game."

"Deal," I said. He ran off to join his class, looking back and waving at me as they trooped out the door. I watched him go and wondered what Will had been like at Duncan's age. I wondered who he would have been if he'd had enough love around him. Whatever happened to Duncan and Riley, I didn't want either of them to end up like Will.

Marcus arrived at the house after work at the same time that I did. I cooked the chicken that had been marinating all day and we ate it with a salad Marcus made and some cheesy breadsticks—Rebecca's latest baking experiment. We both agreed they were a ten out of ten. As we ate, I told him about seeing Duncan and how he was going to help me with my throwing.

"He's a great kid," Marcus said. "I don't understand Lonnie. How can he not come back and be part of those kids' lives?"

"At least he's trying to stay sober," I said. "It's a start. Maybe at some point he can be in their lives in some way."

Marcus broke a breadstick in half and dipped one piece in his salad dressing. "You're nicer than I am."

I smiled. "I don't think so. You just see so many people at their absolute worst that sometimes it colors your perspective."

He smiled at me. "Like I said, nicer."

We finished eating and Marcus cleared the table while I ran water in the sink. I liked washing dishes by hand. I'd been doing it since I was a kid. Sometimes it had been the only way to get a little peace away from my much younger siblings.

"The autopsy results are back," Marcus said.

"And?" I prompted, turning to look at him.

"Will died from a puncture wound to his chest."

I frowned, remembering the stain on Will's sweatshirt that I'd thought might be blood. "What was he stabbed with?"

He shook his head. "I can't tell you that."

I hadn't really expected he would. I turned back to the sink.

"Do you know of any connection between Will and Gerald Hollister?" Marcus asked as he folded the napkins.

I glanced over my shoulder at him. "Why do you think there might be a connection between Duncan and Riley's no-good grandfather and Will Redfern?"

"I think you actually dislike Gerald more than you disliked Will," he said.

"I have good reason to," I said. "Gerald was involved up to his eyeballs when Hope and I ended up at the bottom of that old well. He made himself a deal that meant he only got a slap on the wrist." Hope Lind was Marcus's former partner.

Marcus sighed. "I know. There's no question in my mind that Gerald was way more involved in all of that than he admitted, but we just couldn't prove it."

I turned to look at him. "I know you didn't like that deal."

"If I'd had a bit more time I think I could have found something that would prove Gerald knew exactly what was going on." He pulled a hand over his chin. "It probably would have been better for those kids."

I put a hand on his arm. "It doesn't matter. Lita's taking good care of them. Tell me why you think there may be some kind of connection between Will and Gerald."

"Because Harry saw the two of them talking in the parking lot at Fern's a couple of days before Will's body turned up at the library."

"I take it you've talked to Gerald?"

"Oh yeah."

"So what did he say they were talking about?"

Marcus leaned against the counter. "He said Will wanted to know how Lonnie was doing. They knew each other. From school or something."

I put our glasses in the sink. "I hate to play devil's advocate where Gerald Hollister is concerned, but what reason would he have had to kill Will? Have you found anything that makes you think Gerald was involved in that robbery in some way?"

"It's not possible. The man has an airtight alibi for the night it happened."

"Somebody could be lying for him," I said.

Marcus shook his head. "In this case, I can promise you no one is lying for him. Gerald Hollister was in a poker game at the time of the robbery, with, among other people, Burtis—and my father. He cleaned them out. My father remembers it vividly. He was convinced Gerald was cheating."

I sighed. Burtis Chapman and Elliot Gordon. Two people I knew would not lie for Gerald, or pretty much anyone else.

"I did learn an interesting piece of information about someone else who was on the periphery of the theft, though," Marcus said.

"Interesting in what way?" I asked.

"For a while Hamilton's soon-to-be ex-wife was suspected of being involved in the robbery. She had signed a prenup that was going to restrict how much she would be getting in the divorce."

I nodded. "I read about that but suddenly the story seemed to disappear from the news."

He laced his fingers together and rested his hands on the top of his head. "It seems Mrs. Hamilton was having an affair."

"And her husband found out," I said slowly.

Marcus nodded. "Yes, he did."

"Is it possible Mrs. Hamilton or whoever she was having the affair with or both of them engineered the theft of those paintings?"

"I had the same thought, but Mrs. Hamilton was on a beach in Aruba when the theft took place—with the man she was seeing. He owned the company who was doing some landscaping at the Hamiltons' house."

"Ouch!" I made a face and dumped our knives and forks into the hot, soapy water.

"I know gossip is not a reliable source of information," Marcus said, "but one rumor had it that they were exposed to Hamilton by someone who was working on getting the paintings ready for the exhibit."

Wheels turned in my head. "So maybe the real thief or thieves were trying to deflect suspicion?"

Marcus straightened up, picked up a placemat and shook it in the sink. "It's a possibility, but who knows if the rumor is even true."

"Do you think figuring out who stole those paintings will help you figure out who killed Will?"

He shrugged. "I don't know. At least it's a place to start."

Marcus was going out to help Eddie do some landscaping around the old carriage house. "It's so beautiful inside," I told him, wrapping my arms around his waist. "Thank you."

He kissed me. "I can't wait to marry you."

"You know we have to make some choices about where we're going to live," I said.

"Yeah, I know," he said. "We'll talk about it on the weekend. I really have to get going now."

He kissed me once more and he was gone. I looked down at Hercules and shook my head. "I know a stall when I see one," I said.

"Merow," he said. Apparently, he agreed.

Owen wandered in while I was tidying up the kitchen. He jumped onto one of the chairs and peered at the list of people involved in the theft that I'd taken out of my bag and set on the table. He stretched out a paw and knocked the sheet of paper onto the floor.

"Hey! Don't do that!" I said. I picked him up, set him on the floor and retrieved the sheet of paper at the same time. As I turned back to the counter Owen leaped onto the chair and sent the page floating down to the floor a second time.

I picked him up again and held him at eye level. "Knock it off," I said sternly.

He glared at me. I put him on the floor. He continued to stare pointedly at me. I picked up the list again. "Your brother and I made this list—it's the names of people who were involved in the art exhibit in some way—they're all potential suspects." He continued to look at me. Cat or not, it was a little disconcerting.

"Fine," I said. "I thought you were more of a paws-on-the-ground kind of cat but you're welcome to help me do a little more research."

Once I'd swept the kitchen and gotten a brownie for myself

and a sardine cracker for Owen we started with Hamilton's former wife. Marcus had piqued my curiosity. Very quickly it became obvious that Selena Winters Hamilton had only been a suspect because of the public and very hostile divorce she had been involved in. Hamilton had had to go to court to get Selena out of their house even though they had a prenuptial agreement. She went after a massive amount of child support for their daughter. Robert Hamilton called his wife a spend-thrift who spent more money on her hair than on groceries. Selena countered that he paid more attention to his art collection and classic cars than he did to his child. It all ended abruptly with a quietly worked out and very private settlement and Hamilton swiftly and vehemently denied that his wife had anything to do with the robbery.

Selena died in a car accident three years later. From her obituary I learned that she'd also had an adult daughter from a brief marriage when she was very young. "I think it might be worth trying to find her," I said to Owen.

"Mrrr," he agreed.

It turned out Selena Winters Hamilton had been born in Red Wing. After more digging I discovered that her older daughter, Reese Winters, owned a cottage just outside of Red Wing. She was a nature photographer specializing in birds and disappearing habitats. I called Maggie to see if she by any chance knew the woman.

"I only know her by her work," Maggie said, "which, by the way, is incredible, but Nic might know her. I think I remember him saying one time that they went to school together or something like that."

Nic Sutton was one of the other artists in the co-op. He created assemblages with metal and paper, things most people threw away or hopefully tried to recycle. He worked part-time at Eric's Place, partly, as he explained it, for the money and partly for the socializing. He'd told me once that he felt he'd be a pasty hermit with a three-foot-long beard if he didn't.

"Thanks, Mags," I said. "I'll try to connect with Nic tomorrow."

Owen and I moved on to Jameson Quilleran, an art historian/researcher who had been hired to flesh out the details of the paintings and their histories for the copy in the exhibit's catalog. He was originally from London, England. I was expecting someone in their fifties with a tweedy suit and professorial demeanor. Instead I found a photo of a man in his early forties with short, wavy hair flecked with gray and a couple of days' stubble, wearing jeans and a black shirt with the sleeves rolled back.

"Well, that'll teach me to judge someone by a stereotype," I said to Owen.

He settled on my lap and we read about Jameson Quilleran's education and experience. It appeared that at the moment he was in England, but I knew that didn't mean he couldn't have flown here and then back again. When I took another bite of my brownie Owen somehow took us to another news site, almost as though he'd been waiting for me to be distracted for a moment so he could do that. It was possible he had.

I read the article Owen found and learned that several years ago Quilleran had gotten into an argument with an artist that had gotten physical. The artist's nose had been broken. The art historian had paid a fine and was ordered to take an anger management class. He had been working in Minneapolis at the time.

I leaned back in my chair. Rebecca had told me that Will had been ordered to take a court-mandated anger management class. Was it possible the two men had been in the same class? "Is this too big of a stretch?" I asked Owen.

"Mrrr," he said.

I wasn't sure if that was a yes or a no. Could whatever had led to Will being sentenced to anger management training have made the news? I checked the *Chronicle*'s archives for three months on either side of the theft of the paintings and after a bit of searching found the story. Will had gotten into some kind of argument at a building supply store in Minneapolis with another customer. Like Jameson Quilleran, he had been sentenced to an in-person, six-week anger management class just two days after the art historian. They had both appeared before the same judge in Minneapolis.

"How are we going to find out if they were in the same group?" I said to Owen. "Because I really think they might have been."

He looked at the computer screen. So maybe the answer was somewhere online.

I had noticed that Quilleran seemed to document all of his life on social media. I went back to the time just after he was sentenced and finally found two different photos of him that he captioned "Learning my lesson." The building he was standing in front of was modern and angular with two walls that seemed to be completely made out of glass.

I searched the image of the building behind him and found its location. Bergstrom Associates was located in downtown Minneapolis and they offered an anger management class along with some other programs.

"I knew it," I said to Owen. I held up my hand. "High five."

He looked at me and then at his paw. Overall he seemed confused.

I kissed the top of his head instead. "All we need to do is find out if Will Redfern was in that class as well. How hard can that be?"

chapter 7

Bridget's editorial in Tuesday's edition of the newspaper chided the police for dragging their feet on solving Will Redfern's murder. She seemed to imply they weren't putting in their best effort because Will had just gotten out of prison.

"The case is only a week old," Marcus exclaimed. "We're not miracle workers. It takes time to interview people and gather evidence. Until the autopsy was done we didn't know for certain that Will even was murdered." He exhaled loudly in frustration.

I poured a cup of coffee and handed it to him. "You still haven't figured out how Bridget is getting her information?" I asked.

He shook his head. "No one seems to have any idea." He set his mug on the table and picked up his tablet. "Listen to what she wrote: *If we do not maintain justice, justice will not maintain us.*"

"Francis Bacon," I said softly. I put a hand on his arm. "I know that you're working this case as hard as any other. And so does anyone who knows you. I know it's not easy, but don't let Bridget get to you."

He put an arm around me. "I truly believe that Will deserves justice. I believe everyone does."

I laid my head on his shoulder. "That's why I want to find out who killed him. I believe that Will deserves justice as well, and if there's anything I can do to make that happen I'm going to do it. When I saw Duncan at the library yesterday I thought, Will was a little boy like that once upon a time. I don't believe the kind of person Duncan will grow up to be has already been decided. After all, look at all the changes Riley has made over the last several months. And if it's true for them, then it was true for the little boy Will used to be."

I felt surprisingly emotional thinking about Will as a child. "There's no one speaking up for him—not even Bridget, really; she's just stirring things up to sell newspapers. I know it doesn't really make sense but I can't let the person who killed Will get away with it."

"You know I'd rather you stay out of this," Marcus said.

"I know."

"Is there any point in me trying to talk you out of it?"

I shook my head. "Riley has made some mistakes. I asked

people not to give up on her, to give her a second chance. I'd be a hypocrite if I didn't at least try to find out who killed Will. I know you didn't like it but I was going to give him a second chance. For me that doesn't go away just because he's dead."

Marcus kissed the top of my head. "The only thing I'll say is please be careful."

"I will," I said. "Both Will and Jameson Quilleran were ordered to take part in an anger management program. It's possible they were in the same one."

"Seems like a bit of a stretch," Marcus said.

I shrugged. "We'll see."

I left early so I could stop in at the café. Nic was working, which was what I'd been hoping. I handed over my travel mug. "We have rhubarb scones," he said as he reached for the coffeepot.

I smiled. "I think I'm going to need to try one of those."

Nic finished filling my mug and handed it back to me. "I'll grab you one from the kitchen," he said.

He returned with a small wax paper bag. I could smell cinnamon and nutmeg.

"Thanks," I said.

"Could I get you anything else?" Nic asked.

"Maybe," I said. "Maggie said you might know a photographer named Reese Winters. She's based in Red Wing at least part of the time."

He nodded. "I know Reese."

"I'd like to talk to her."

His expression became guarded. "About what?" he asked.

"You've probably heard a fair amount of talk that a painting at the library may very well have been stolen."

"I've heard some things." His tone was noncommittal.

"I'd like to talk to Reese about that painting. It may belong to a man named Robert Hamilton. Her mother was married to him. Would you be willing to give her my number?" I held out a slip of paper. "That's all I'm asking."

Nic hesitated for a moment and then he took the paper from me.

"I'll give Reese your number," he said. "I can't promise she'll call you."

"That's fine," I said. "Thank you." I paid for my coffee and scone and headed back to the truck crossing my fingers—literally and figuratively—that this would work.

Marcus showed up at the library just a couple of minutes before eleven with Anita Marler. She was short, barely five feet high, with dark hair that just brushed her shoulders and dark eyes. She had confirmed what Ruby had suspected. The watercolor was Robert Hamilton's missing painting.

"Thank you for coming," I said. "I know the chances of having another valuable painting here are almost nil."

"I'm happy to look at everything for you," she said. "In my experience some very valuable pieces of art have been found in a lot stranger places than this."

"Do you mind if I ask where?" I said.

"Not at all. Beehive. Goat shed. Mattress. Huge bag of oatmeal." She ticked each one off on her fingers.

"Excuse me," I said. "Goat shed?"

Anita nodded. "Under a fairly substantial pile of goat excrement. The painting was wrapped in several layers of plastic. Sadly that didn't really help with the smell."

"Well, our paintings have just been kept in a couple of boxes in our workroom," I said. "No goats. Or bees. Possibly a few dust bunnies."

Marcus offered to wait for Anita and drive her back to the bed-and-breakfast where she was staying. She thanked him and explained that she was meeting someone for lunch at Eric's Place, and since it was such a nice day she wanted to walk. She told him she'd talk to him tomorrow and he left.

We started by walking around the main floor of the library. Anita took a close look at every painting we had hanging on the walls. Occasionally she asked what I knew about the backstory of a piece. Once she'd looked at everything out on display I took her upstairs. The two boxes of paintings were on a table in the workroom. She took each piece of artwork out of the box, one at a time, and checked it carefully. "I do like this one," she said, holding up Daniel Gunnerson's window painting. "A local artist, I'm guessing."

I nodded. "And funeral director."

She raised an eyebrow, but all she said was, "He has a good eye for color and perspective."

In the end, none of the paintings in our so-called collection were valuable. "It doesn't mean they aren't a pleasure to look at, though," Anita said.

"You worked on getting Robert Hamilton's paintings ready for the exhibit, didn't you?" I asked.

"I worked on checking their provenance, yes. You understand what that is?"

I nodded. "What is the difference between what you were doing and what Jameson Quilleran was doing?"

"I guess the best way to describe it is my job was to determine each of the paintings was legitimate, that none of them were fakes or had been altered in any way. It's similar to the way the police have to be able to document the chain of custody of a piece of evidence. Does that make sense?"

"It does," I said.

"Jameson's job was to write the story of each painting—when did the artist create it, who owned it, where had it been exhibited? Sometimes our work overlapped."

I started putting the paintings back in the boxes. "Do you mind me asking what led you to a career in art?"

"I think it's probably in my DNA," she said, handing me one of the canvases. "My mother was a history teacher and my father was the proverbial struggling artist. He painted oceans and riverscapes—beautiful but ultimately very bleak. He never found much of a following. His work was considered too unsettling."

A hint of a smile played across her face. "Ironically now, almost ten years after his death, his work is developing a following stemming, it seems, from one of his paintings being in the background in a scene from a Netflix show. It was only visible for a few seconds but that was all it took."

She took out a business card and handed it to me. "Here's my number. If anything else turns up and you have questions please get in touch with me."

I thanked her and reminded her to send me an invoice for her time.

She shook her head. "As far I'm concerned this is part of the police investigation and I'm already being compensated for that."

We walked downstairs and I went outside with Anita to give her directions to the café. Harry was just getting out of his truck. Boris was on the passenger side. I could see his tail wagging as he looked at me through the windshield.

"Oh, what a beautiful dog," Anita exclaimed.

"That's Boris," I said. "Would you like to say hello?"

She smiled. "Please."

We walked over to the truck. Harry was getting a box out of the back. I introduced the two of them. "Could we say hello to Boris?" I asked.

"Don't see why not," Harry said. He opened the passenger door of the truck and the dog jumped out. He came right over to me, tail wagging. I bent down to give the top of his head a scratch. After a moment he turned to look at Anita, head tipped to one side in curiosity. She held out her hand and he sniffed it, then nudged it with his head.

"He likes you," I said as she stroked his fur.

"He's so gentle," Anita said.

"Been that way since he was a pup," Harry said. "His mother had the same temperament."

Anita smiled at Harry. "Thank you for letting me meet Boris," she said. She gave the dog one last scratch behind his ear.

Harry opened the passenger door of the truck. "C'mon," he said to the dog. "Some of us have to get a little work done." The dog made a low sound like a sigh but he climbed back into the truck again.

I thanked Harry, and then Anita and I walked over to the sidewalk. I gave her directions to the café. She glanced over her shoulder at Harry's truck. "What a great dog," she said. She looked at me. "I'm a dog person. And a cat person."

"Cat person here," I said, holding up one hand, "with a lot of exceptions for my favorite dogs."

"Do you have cats?" Anita asked.

"I have two. Owen is a gray tabby and Hercules is a tuxedo cat. A lot of the time they think they're people."

She laughed. "In my experience most cats are that way."

"It's been a pleasure to meet you," I said. "Thank you for looking at all of our artwork."

"I enjoyed meeting you, too," she said. "And please, if you have any more questions, call me."

I assured her I would and she headed off down the sidewalk.

I spent my lunch break eating a turkey sandwich I'd brought from home and trying to track down the guys who worked for/with Will. I most wanted to talk to Eddie Nystrom. He and Will had seemed like they were friends outside of work. I was hoping Eddie or maybe one of the others might know something about Will's stint in that anger management class, assuming they would even talk to me at all. I had no luck. Not one of the men seemed to have any social media and I couldn't locate so much as a street address for any of them.

I was just coming down the stairs when a man who looked vaguely familiar walked into the building. He was in his early-to-mid-fifties with short salt-and-pepper hair. He wore a dark suit with a black shirt and a black-and-gray tie. Both the clothing and the way he moved said confidence, and money. He stopped to speak to Susan at the desk and she pointed in my direction. He was an inch or two under six feet but he seemed taller and he had what my actor/director mother would call presence.

"Ms. Paulson," he said as I walked toward him. His voice was deep with a slight rasp to it. "I'm Robert Hamilton. Detective Gordon told me I'd find you here."

Robert Hamilton. That's why he looked familiar. I'd seen a couple of photos of a younger version of the man online. His hair was much shorter now and he was wearing glasses, which was probably why I hadn't recognized him right away.

"Welcome to the library, Mr. Hamilton," I said. "What can I do for you?"

He smiled. "I wanted to thank you for the return of my painting."

"I'm sorry no one realized what we had for so long."

"I'm just grateful I'm getting my property back," he said. He looked around. "I'd like to learn more about your library, Ms. Paulson. Would you have time to give me a tour?"

Behind his back Susan, who had been unashamedly eavesdropping, seemed to be doing semaphore with a Post-it Note. She'd drawn a dollar sign on the yellow slip of paper. I was pretty sure she wanted me to say yes.

I smiled. "I do have time and I'd be happy to give you a tour." We started in the computer room. I explained how we'd had a fund-raiser to replace our ancient machines with the new ones the space now boasted. I showed off the trim that Oren had carefully replicated to replace the pieces that had been damaged by water and time.

Hamilton asked questions about our usage numbers and reader demographics. I talked about the various programs we ran, including Reading Buddies, which I had a soft spot for.

"You have a rather eclectic collection of artwork," he said.

"Most of it predates my tenure here," I said. "You know Anita Marler."

He nodded. "I do."

"She was here this morning. She looked at all of the paintings we have. There was nothing valuable among them."

He pointed at one of my favorites, cats playing poker. "It may not be valuable but I do like that one," he said. "Usually it's dogs."

"Mr. Hamilton, is Will Redfern's name familiar to you?" I asked. I wasn't really sure why Hamilton wanted a tour of the library, but I wasn't letting the chance to ask some questions pass by.

He straightened the left cuff of his suit jacket. I thought about how many large-print books I could buy for the seniors with what he'd probably spent on that suit. "It's not," he said. "Detective Gordon asked the same question. He also showed me the man's photo. I didn't recognize his face, either." He looked up at the plaster medallion on the ceiling. "Mr. Redfern did some of the restoration work on this building."

I nodded. "Yes, he did." It seemed Hamilton had done a little digging into Will's background.

"He also assaulted you."

"He did that as well," I said, making an effort to keep the emotion out of my voice.

"To be frank, Will Redfern didn't sound like a very nice person."

To my surprise I suddenly felt defensive of Will. "He still didn't deserve what happened to him."

Hamilton smiled then. "Thank you for your time, Ms. Paulson," he said. His eyes were the color of a cup of chocolaty cocoa. They should have looked warm, but they didn't. "And thank you for taking care of my painting. I would like to make a donation to the library as a thank-you."

"It's not necessary," I said. "We didn't do anything. As I told you, we had no idea what we had."

"Nonetheless, I'm grateful and I'd like to express that."

I gave him my most gracious smile. "Thank you, then. You could make a donation to the Reading Buddies program."

"That sounds like an excellent idea."

I felt as though we were trying to out-polite each other. He said he would be in touch and he left.

I walked over to the desk.

"He was very charming," Susan said.

I agreed that he was. I didn't say I thought Robert Hamilton had an edge that he tried to keep covered with his expensive suits and impeccable manners.

Because my parents were actors I'd learned a lot about human nature and what makes people tick by watching them create characters over the years. "Mr. Hamilton wants to give the library a donation as a thank-you," I said.

Susan nudged her cat's-eye glasses up her nose. "I hope you didn't discourage that." Susan was a drop-dead practical person.

I smiled. "I suggested Reading Buddies."

She nodded approvingly. "Excellent choice. Now let's hope that it's a large thank-you."

Maggie called late in the afternoon. "Do you have supper plans?" she asked. She sounded a little frazzled.

"Just spaghetti with Owen and Hercules," I said. "Do you have a better suggestion?"

"How about Eric's lasagna with me? I can't say I'll be as good company as the furballs, though. There was a water pipe leak in my studio and Ruby's, and I've spent most of the day cleaning up."

"Lasagna with you sounds good," I said. "And you're always good company." I had a pair of yoga pants and a T-shirt in my office from a lunchtime yoga class I'd tried a couple of weeks ago so I wouldn't need to go home before tai chi.

I called Marcus, hoping he could check in on Owen and Hercules. "I can do that," he said.

"Robert Hamilton was here earlier," I said.

"He said he wanted to thank you. I'm sorry I didn't get a chance to call and warn you. I was called into a meeting literally right after he left the police station." He paused for a moment. "What did you think of the man?"

"He can be very . . . charming."

"I noticed that."

"I think he only shows what he wants people to know about

him," I said. "I have a feeling he's not someone you would want to play poker with."

"I noticed that as well," Marcus said.

Maggie was waiting at Eric's at our favorite table in the window. We both ordered the lasagna, with tea for Mags and decaf for me. While we waited for our food we talked about the wedding.

"Roma and I are going out to Ella's on Friday to try on our dresses," Maggie said.

"I'm trying my dress on Saturday," I said. I made a mental note to make sure the time didn't conflict with Duncan's baseball game.

"I'm pulling weeds on Saturday." She looked at me over her cup of tea and smiled.

"By any chance are you pulling up weeds around the carriage house?" I asked.

"As a matter of fact, I am. Brady and I are helping with the landscaping."

"Thank you," I said, reaching across the table to give her hand a squeeze. "It's going to be beautiful, but you know I would have married Marcus in the carriage house the way it was."

Maggie laughed. "We all know that, but we also want you to have something just a little nicer."

"Everyone has put so much work into the carriage house."

"Eddie has been very good at getting us all organized. He set up a group chat."

"Eddie's good at a lot of things," I said, taking a sip of my coffee. "He's a real Renaissance man."

"And Riley Hollister has helped a lot," Maggie said. "She's a great kid. She came early on Sunday to help us get all the tables set up. She was Eddie's sous chef in the kitchen. And she spent a whole Saturday afternoon painting in the carriage house." Maggie shook her head. "Of all of us I think she was the only one whose painting skills were up to Roma's standards."

"Roma has been good for Riley," I said.

Maggie smiled. "You've been good for Riley." She took another sip of her tea and frowned.

The front door opened then and Burtis walked in. He stopped at the counter to talk to Claire—giving her an order I guessed.

An idea began to take shape in my head. "Mags, I need to talk to Burtis for a minute," I said.

Maggie was peering into her teapot. "Sure," she said, waving a hand vaguely in my direction.

Burtis smiled when he spotted me.

Burtis Chapman was a big block of a man, barrel-chested and wide shouldered. His face was weathered from all the time he'd spent working outside. He owned several businesses; most of them were one hundred percent legal. He and Marcus's father had been friends their whole life and could get in way more trouble together than they did apart. Burtis was well-read and very smart, although he wasn't above playing the country hick if it served his purposes.

"I saw the carriage house for the first time on the weekend and I heard that you're one of the reasons it looks so spectacular," I said.

"Oh, did you now?" He arched an eyebrow at me.

I hugged him. "Thank you," I said.

"I didn't do much. Mostly I just looked at Eddie and Harrison's plans and told 'em what I thought of them."

I knew Burtis had done a lot more than that and I knew he wasn't going to take any more of a thank-you than I had already given him.

"I heard about Will Redfern's body turning up in your library," Burtis said. "I'm sorry about that. My grandmother used to say you lay down with dogs, you get up with fleas, and as much as I hate to say it, that seems to apply to Will. He couldn't seem to stay away from trouble."

"Do you know what happened to the guys who worked for Will once he went to jail?" I asked.

"Far as I know they went to work for other people. Not here in town, because fair or not they were all tarred with the same brush as Will. Why are you askin'?"

"I'm just curious."

His dark eyes narrowed. "I'm sure you are, but those are not people you need to have anything to do with."

Claire came out from the kitchen then with two large

brown paper bags. She set them on the counter in front of Burtis. He paid for the food and as he turned around Maggie waved hello. He smiled back at her. His expression became serious again as he turned back to me. "My grandmother had a lot of sayings about dogs, you know. 'Let sleeping dogs lie' was another one she used a lot."

It was impossible to miss his point.

"You take care of yourself, Kathleen," he said.

I nodded. "You too."

I walked back to the table wondering how I was going to find Will's men now.

chapter 8

Claire brought over our lasagna and a new pot of tea for Maggie. As we ate we talked about ideas for next year's Winterfest celebration.

"They should have had a theme a month ago but they're still debating," Maggie said. "Are you interested in hosting a workshop or two at the library?"

"Yes," I said. We'd done workshops with the artists' co-op before. They were always popular. I took a bite of the lasagna and gave a little sigh of happiness.

"I'm thinking about some kind of watercolor class for adults and Ruby's trying to convince Nic to do a workshop for kids all about making art from found objects."

"Those would both go over well," I said, "especially the class for kids."

"Have you found any more valuable paintings?" Maggie asked with a grin.

"Not unless you think cats playing poker could be valuable. So far no one else does."

"Value is like beauty," she said, gesturing with her fork. "It's in the eye of the beholder."

"I've still gotta go with no on the cats," I said.

Maggie took another bite of her lasagna. "Do you think Will could have had anything to do with the theft of that painting?"

"I do, but Marcus doesn't."

"So what have you come up with so far?"

I frowned. "What do mean?"

"I know you," she said. "Will's body was found in the library. I know you didn't like him very much, but you're not going to do nothing, either."

I set my fork down and reached for my coffee. "There may, *may* be a connection between Will and someone who was working on the exhibit."

"So it is possible Will was involved somehow in that painting ending up at the library? What would have been in it for him?"

"I don't know. You know the kind of person he was. Will was always looking for the easy score. I don't have any proof, but I can't shake the feeling he was involved somehow with the theft of Robert Hamilton's artwork. I know that seems far-fetched, but so does the idea that he wasn't but he somehow decided to steal the one painting in the building that was actually valuable."

"You'll figure it out," Maggie said with more confidence in her voice than I felt. "You always do."

We finished eating, declined Claire's tempting suggestions for dessert and walked down to the tai chi studio. Maggie worked us hard in class and it felt good to concentrate on moving my body and not think about Will Redfern and stolen paintings for a while.

The next morning I called Larry Taylor and asked him to come take a look at the library's alarm system. It still bothered me that Will had managed to get into the building so easily.

"I'm not an alarm technician so I'm not sure how I can help," Larry said. "Have you talked to the alarm company?"

"I called them as soon as we got back into the building. They sent someone over. He found nothing and did a reset but I keep thinking they missed something. I trust you to be honest with me. Maybe I am just overreacting."

"Maybe," Larry said, "and maybe not. I have some time right after lunch. I'll see you then."

I thanked him and we said good-bye. Maybe I was finally getting somewhere.

Ruby showed up mid-morning with two more boxes of

things for the yard sale. "Burtis will be dropping by with some tables at some point and I'm going to get the kids in on the weekend to start sorting and pricing if that's okay."

"That's fine with me," I said. I loved how enthusiastic the kids were about raising money to get books for other kids.

I spent my lunch break online once more, looking for more information about the various people who were suspects in the early days after the robbery. Anita Marler volunteered a lot of her time at an animal shelter. She was a strong supporter of using cruelty-free products, so much so that she seemed to support a break-in at a company that was still testing some of its products on animals. Given how taken she had been with Boris, I wasn't surprised. Jameson Quilleran spent a lot of his free time partying in various London clubs. Both of the security guards seemed to be retired. One of them, Terry Long, was breeding German shepherds. I managed to find a phone number for the other one, Alphonse Dupont. I called the number and got his voice mail. I left a message and crossed my fingers he'd call me back.

I wasn't sure what I was looking for exactly—it's not like someone would post their plans for stealing artwork on their social media pages. I sighed and leaned back in my chair. Maybe I needed some help from Hercules. More than once he'd randomly taken us someplace where I'd learned an important piece of information.

Larry showed up just after one o'clock. He was built like his big brother Harry, but he had blond hair and green eyes. Larry examined the alarm pad and the door and reiterated that he was no expert on this kind of thing.

"I know you'll do your best and that's more than good enough for me," I said. "If anyone can figure this out you can."

Larry laughed. "But no pressure," he said.

I was running an update on one of our community computers almost an hour later—and marveling how easy it was to do with the new machines—when Larry approached me. The look on his face—a mix of satisfaction and trouble—told me he'd found something.

"You were right," he said.

"You found something?"

He held out his hand. On his palm was a small box, no bigger than a white plastic pencil eraser. It had coated wires coming out of the top and the bottom with metal alligator clips on the ends. "It's actually rather ingenious. The alarm is wired into the building but it also has a battery backup."

I nodded. "In case the power goes out."

"There's a five-second delay between the power going off and the battery taking over," Larry said. "When it's activated this little device interrupts the circuit and makes it seem like the power has gone off and in those five seconds the alarm doesn't work."

"But five seconds can't be enough time to unlock the door and get inside," I said.

"Oh, it's more than enough. All Will would have needed was this little magic box and a key to the door."

Abigail had misplaced her keys the day before Will was killed. Maybe she hadn't dropped them. Maybe Will had swiped them and then later pushed them under the printer stand to be found. That would explain how he'd gotten a key to the door. Will—or someone who was helping him—had copied Abigail's key. As for the alarm, I'd had a gut feeling there was something off about the system but I would have never guessed it would be something like this. "Could Will have done this by himself?" I asked.

"Easily. As long as he knew where to put this"—Larry held up the device—"he could have triggered it remotely. Will knew the library well. Do you know if he had been in the building before the night he died?"

I nodded. "Yes, he had."

"He probably slipped downstairs and put it in place then. I think we should call Marcus before I do anything else."

"I think you're right," I said. It was a much more logical reason for Will showing up here than him wanting to talk to me.

Marcus arrived about fifteen minutes later. Larry explained what he'd found and showed Marcus where the device had been connected to the alarm system.

"I don't know how long the box was there but I can say for certain it hasn't been there more than a month because I was in the building working about four weeks ago and I wouldn't have missed it."

Unlike the technician from the alarm company, I thought.

"Does that thing have any legitimate use?" Marcus asked.

Larry shrugged. "Not that I know of, but your tech people should be able to give you a better idea." He looked at me. "I don't want to overstep but you might want to think about changing alarm companies, because the technician they sent out should have noticed this."

I rubbed the back of my neck with one hand. "You're not overstepping at all," I said. "I was thinking the same thing."

"A buddy of mine runs a security company in Red Wing. I'm not trying to recruit business for a friend, but Ron is a good guy and he'll treat you fairly. I have his card in my truck if you'd like it, no pressure."

"I would like it, please," I said.

Larry went out to the parking lot.

"You were right," Marcus said. "Somehow Will is or was connected to the theft of those paintings. Things don't make sense otherwise."

"I know," I said. "I just wish I could find the connection."

He smiled. "Are you going to say I told you so?"

"No. Before today there was no concrete evidence that Will was involved." I held up my thumb and index finger about half an inch apart and smiled. "I might be thinking it, though, just a little."

"Maybe we'll get lucky and find a fingerprint on this thing." He had put the device inside an evidence bag. "I'm going to send someone over to take a look around the electrical panel as well to look for Will's prints. It's been so long since he worked on the building, they shouldn't be here anywhere."

I walked Marcus to the door. Larry was just coming in from outside.

"I might have some questions for you later," Marcus said to Larry.

He nodded. "Not a problem. Give me a call anytime."

Marcus left.

"If you don't mind I'll take a quick look around the building just to make sure Will didn't leave any other surprises," Larry said.

"If you have the time, honestly, I'd feel better," I said. "And make sure you send me an invoice for your time."

"Hey, I just took a quick look around. You don't have to pay me for that."

"The alarm company sent a bill and didn't do half as good a job. Send me an invoice."

Larry grinned and shook his head. "It's kind of hard to grow up with the old man and be half-assed about anything." He handed over the business card he'd gotten from his truck. "Ron will do right by you."

"I'll call him. It'll probably be tomorrow before I get the chance. We need to do something about this alarm system. If I can get an estimate from your friend fairly quickly, I can run it by the board at their next meeting."

"Once Ron has a look around it won't take him long to make a recommendation," Larry said. "And he won't try to upsell you."

"I'm very grateful for both you and Georgia," I said. "You

know, she did a wonderful job with the cupcakes at the shower."

"She and Emmy had a great time making them." He smiled. "You'll like being married, Kathleen. I sure as hell do. I went from being on my own to having a wife and a daughter and I had no idea I had so many empty spaces in my life until they filled them. Emmy wants a brother or a sister, you know."

"She'd be a great big sister."

"Yeah, she would," Larry said. He put a hand over his heart. "And how could more love be bad?" He gestured over his shoulder. "I'll go see if there's anything to find. It shouldn't take me very long."

The crime scene tech arrived just a few minutes later, and before he left Larry showed her where he'd found the device in the basement. He hadn't found anything amiss in the rest of the building. I was glad I'd followed my instincts and called him.

It was busy for the rest of the afternoon. I helped a mother find several picture books with characters wearing glasses for her daughter who had just gotten a pair and wasn't happy having to wear them. I showed three teenage boys how to choose "actual, like, real" books for an essay and I answered a question about formatting a bibliography, something that was usually Mary's bailiwick.

"Thank you," Susan said. "It's been a long time since I formatted an essay. Back when I was in school we had to carve it all onto stone tablets."

When I left at the end of the day Burtis's truck was in the

parking lot and he was standing by the front bumper. There was someone with him, a big barrel-chested man with a bald head, wearing jeans, work boots and a dusty black T-shirt with the logo of a local microbrewery on the front. His hands were jammed in his pockets but I knew one of them was big enough to pretty much cover my head.

It was Eddie Nystrom.

chapter 9

Burtis had found Eddie Nystrom.

How? And given what he'd said to me at the café, why?

I walked over to them. "Hello, Burtis," I said. "I didn't expect to see you here."

"I'm sorry to stop in when you're about to head home for the night," he said, "but I happened to bump into Eddie here, and given everything that had happened with Will, I thought you might have a few questions, and it turned out that Eddie just happened to have some free time right now."

Somehow I doubted Eddie was standing there completely voluntarily. Burtis didn't like to hear no. Not that he heard it very often.

"How have you been, Eddie?" I asked.

His hands were jammed in his pockets. "Pretty good, I guess. I swear I didn't know that Will was going to break into your library."

"Did you know he was back in town?"

He nodded. "Yeah, well pretty much everybody knew that. He wasn't exactly hiding or anything. I mean he did his time and all." He darted a quick look Burtis's way.

"Had you seen Will?"

Eddie scratched the back of his neck with one massive hand. "That kinda depends on what you mean by seen."

Eddie could be very literal, I remembered.

"Did you talk to the man?" Burtis asked.

Eddie shook his head. "No, sir, but I was out at The Brick and I saw Will across the room talking to some guy."

Burtis glanced at me and then turned his attention to Eddie again. "What guy?" he said.

Eddie shrugged and shifted restlessly from one foot to the other. It was obvious he would rather be anywhere other than standing here talking to me with Burtis watching him like a hawk eyeing a field mouse. "I dunno. The guy's back was to me and he didn't turn around so I never did see his face."

"Do you know what they were talking about?" I asked.

"Not a clue. I was too far away but it seemed to be pretty darn serious because Will had that look on his face he used to get when something pissed him off."

I shifted the strap of my messenger bag up higher on my

shoulder. "Eddie, do you know why Will might have wanted to break into the library?"

Eddie scratched his neck again. "I hadn't talked to Will in years. How am I supposed to know that?"

"You mean to say you haven't heard anything?" Burtis asked.

"Well, people say things but that doesn't mean they're true."

I had forgotten how frustrating it was to talk to any of the guys who had worked for Will. They were all masters at never really answering a question.

"What are people saying?" I asked.

Eddie shrugged. "It might just be a lot of loose talk. You know how people are."

"Answer the lady's question, Eddie," Burtis said. There was an edge of warning in his voice.

"People were saying that Will had figured out some kind of score, some way to make a lot of money. But I don't see how it coulda had anything to do with that painting he was supposed to be tryin' to steal from you."

"Why do you think that?" I said.

His hands stayed jammed in his pockets but his chin came up. "I don't mean to talk trash about Will, because he's dead and all, but what the heck did he know about paintings? Squat, that's what. And second of all, you're smart. You went to college and all. If someone was going to figure out that there's some painting in the library worth a truckload of money, wouldn't it be you and not Will? And how the hell would some painting have gotten there anyway?" He gestured at the building. "That's a library, not an art gallery."

He wasn't going to answer many more questions, I realized, even with Burtis standing there. "Eddie, do you remember Will getting arrested for something that happened in the parking lot of a building supply store in Minneapolis about six months or so before you all started working on the library?"

His expression darkened. "Yeah, I remember that. In fact, I was there. Guy was an asshole. 'Scuse my language. What happened wasn't Will's fault. He was just trying to get the truck loaded and we would have been done in maybe five minutes but this jerk wouldn't stop going on about how the one-ton had him blocked in. All he needed to do was chill and go drink his girly coffee." Eddie gave a snort of laughter. "I was surprised Will kept his cool as long as he did and didn't pop the guy sooner."

"The judge sentenced Will to anger management classes."

"Yeah, he did," Eddie said. "But it was the jerk who provoked Will who should have been made to take a class. Like I said, all the dude had to do was wait five freakin' minutes." He shook his head in disgust.

I had a headache. I wanted to go home and have supper but I wanted answers more than that. "Do you know where Will went for his class?"

Eddie shook his head.

My heart sank.

"It was somewhere in Minneapolis with some shrink. I

dropped Will off a couple of times—Lord, what a butt-ugly building. It was on the corner with all glass on the two sides and some of the windows stuck out over the sidewalk."

I remembered the building I had seen on Jameson Quilleran's social media. I tried not to show my excitement. "Thanks for talking to me, Eddie," I said. "I really appreciate it."

He glanced at Burtis. "Hey, well, you know, it's not a big deal."

"Got any more questions, Kathleen?" Burtis asked.

I shook my head. "Thank you for bringing Eddie by."

"I'll be back with some tables for Ruby," he said. "Tomorrow, likely."

Eddie opened the passenger door of the truck, then he hesitated. "Miss Paulson, I know you didn't like Will and I know Will gave you reasons not to like him, but he wasn't a totally bad guy."

I pressed my lips together, nodded but didn't say a word. Eddie got into the truck.

"You get what you needed?" Burtis said.

I nodded. "I think I did. Thank you."

"Good," he said. "You have a good night." He climbed in his truck and drove off.

I got into in my own truck and headed up the hill for home. When I came around the side of the house I found Hercules sitting on the back stoop with Fifi, the Justasons' dog, perched beside him. Fifi lived next door. And despite what the name suggested, Fifi was a male dog. Over the past several months he and Hercules had forged an odd kind of friendship. Fifi used to be afraid of Hercules and still gave other cats, including Owen, a wide berth, but I often came home to the two of them in the yard together.

"Hello," I said.

"Mrr," Hercules replied.

"I'll be right back," I told him.

I took Fifi by the collar. "It's very nice to see you, but it's suppertime and you need to go home." I headed next door to the Justasons', where I could hear the boys outside. They saw me coming and Ronan ran over to get the dog from me.

"Sorry," he said. "Fifi got loose somehow. I think he figured out how to open the gate to the backyard." He gave me a guileless smile. I had a feeling that child was going to run the world someday.

"I'm sure that's what it was," I said. I gave Fifi one more scratch on the head and headed back to the house.

Hercules was waiting in the porch now that he didn't have company, sitting on the bench as usual. He jumped down and waited for me to open the kitchen door for a change.

Marcus had a practice with the ball team so I decided to make myself chicken sausage with apples and leeks for supper. Both cats wandered in and out while I was cooking. "Don't waste your 'I'm so hungry and cute' looks on me because neither one of you are getting any sausage," I told them.

Owen went down into the basement to sulk, making little grumbling noises all the way down the stairs, while Hercules just positioned himself closer to my chair. Owen was still in the basement when I finished the dishes.

"For all we know, your brother could be plotting world domination down there," I said. Hercules yawned. Either he didn't think it was likely or he didn't care.

I got my laptop and brought up the photos of the building where Jameson Quilleran had gone for his anger management class. I was certain that Eddie had described the same building. What were the chances there were two structures in Minneapolis that fit the description? Will Redfern and Jameson Quilleran had gone to the same anger management class. It was the connection between Will and the painting. It had to be.

"All we need to do now is to figure out how the painting got to the library in the first place," I said to the cat, "and who killed Will."

My phone rang. I didn't recognize the number, but the area code was from this part of the state.

It was Reese Winters.

"Nic Sutton gave me your message," she said. "Would you be able to come to me to talk?" Her voice was low and quiet.

"Absolutely," I said.

"I'm available this weekend." I remembered Duncan's ball game and my dress fitting on Saturday and suggested sometime early on Sunday. We settled on Sunday morning.

We agreed to meet at a coffee shop in Red Wing. I thanked her and we ended the call. "This could be interesting," I said to Hercules.

Marcus stopped in on his way home after practice. I told him what I'd learned from Eddie and from Jameson Quilleran's social media.

"You know it's not definitive proof that they knew each other or even were in the same group," he said.

"It's enough for me," I said. I reached across the table for his hand and intertwined my fingers with his. "I'm changing the subject now."

He smiled. "To what?"

"To the fact that you keep avoiding talking about where we're going to live once we're married."

"I'm not avoiding talking about it," he said. "We have lots of time to work that out."

Hercules meowed loudly.

"You can't even sell that to a cat," I said.

He shook his head. "Okay, fine. I hate to make you give up your home here. I know how much you love this house." He made a sweeping gesture with one hand. "But I don't think it makes sense to give up my house. You're just renting and I own my place—at least the bank and I own it. The mortgage payments are reasonable. Everett could decide to do something else with this house at any time."

I nodded. "You're right," I said.

He looked surprised. "But you'll miss Rebecca and Fifi and your garden. Not to mention, how will Owen and Hercules adjust?"

"So you'd live here just to make my two cats happy?"

He smiled and rubbed his thumb along the back of my hand. "Well when you say it out loud it sounds a bit silly, but yes, I would because it would make you happy."

"Owen and Hercules will adjust." Hercules was sitting at my feet. He looked skeptical.

"You will," I told him. I looked at Marcus. "Home is where you and the three furballs are."

"You don't have to make a final decision right this moment," he said. He leaned over and kissed me. It wasn't until after he was gone that I realized we still hadn't actually settled anything.

chapter 10

Hercules and I were both restless after Marcus left. I went outside and Herc came out to sit on the stoop next to me. I looked around the backyard and it hit me that soon I could be living somewhere else. I had a bit of a sinking feeling in my chest. I really did want to stay in this house, even though I thought Marcus was right. It made more sense for the cats and me to move to his house. He had more space. He had equity.

Hercules leaned against me as though he understood how conflicted I felt. "Marcus's house doesn't have Rebecca or Everett," I said. "I won't be able to walk to tai chi class."

He meowed his agreement.

"It doesn't have Fifi next door. They don't decorate for

Christmas out where Marcus lives the way they do here." Hercules made a soft sound like a sigh.

That was exactly how I felt. I picked him up and went back inside.

I decided a cup of hot chocolate would help. As Roma liked to remind me, chocolate or duct tape could fix pretty much any problem, which was why she almost always had both with her.

I stretched and leaned against the counter while I waited for the milk to heat. "I don't want to talk about where we're going to live," I said to Hercules. "I'd rather talk about Will." I held up one finger. "So what do we know? Number one, we know Will and Jameson Quilleran were in the same anger management class."

Hercules tipped his head to one side and meowed at me.

"You're as bad as Marcus," I said. "Fine. I strongly *suspect* the two of them were in the same class."

That seemed to satisfy him.

"So, number two, we can infer that they talked to each other."

Hercules seemed to consider the idea and after a moment meowed with a fair amount of enthusiasm, which I decided to see as agreement. He looked up at my laptop. I realized I didn't have a number three.

"Want to see what else we can find about Jameson Quilleran?" I asked.

He jumped up onto a chair and put one paw on the edge of the table. He was in.

Our search didn't yield much more information about the art historian. For all of his social media, his posts were very superficial.

I slumped back in the chair while Hercules continued to stare at the computer screen. "Anita Marler said she was staying in town for a few days. Maybe I should see what she can tell me about Mr. Quilleran."

"Mrrr," Hercules said. I had the feeling he wasn't paying the slightest bit of attention to me. In other words, he was very much being a cat.

It was raining hard on Thursday morning. Owen woke me up early by rubbing his face against my cheek. I opened my eyes and sneezed, which startled him and sent him toppling over onto the carpet.

I looked over the side of the bed. "Are you all right?" I asked.

He shook himself, looking a little shame-faced.

I sneezed again, and when I glanced down at the floor a second time, Owen had disappeared. Literally or figuratively, I wasn't sure.

I wore my new rain boots with the cat paw prints all over them and my big yellow slicker down to the library. Mary got dropped off by her husband and walked over to join me at the bottom of the steps holding a huge striped umbrella over her head.

"One of the first things I'm going to do this morning is call Larry's friend about the alarm system," I said to Mary as I shut off the alarm and unlocked the front door.

Mary shook her head. "What's the world coming to when a library needs an alarm system?" She shot me a sideways glance. "Yes, I know that makes me sound as old as Noah."

"Maybe not Noah," I teased. "Maybe one of his kids."

We headed inside, turned on the lights and took a quick look at the book drop. It was full as usual. We went upstairs and I dropped my things in my office while Mary went to start the coffee.

Once Abigail had arrived and the building was open I called Larry's friend Ron.

"Larry gave me a heads-up that you might call," he said.

I gave him a brief rundown of what had happened.

"The company you've been using had always done good work," Ron said, "but it was sold, about a year ago, to a much bigger firm, and in the changeover some things have fallen through the cracks."

"Could you come and take a look at our system?" I glanced out the window over my shoulder. It was still raining hard.

"I have to be in Mayville Heights after lunch and I could stop in later in the afternoon—somewhere between three and three thirty. Or if that's too short notice for you, I could come next Tuesday morning."

"This afternoon will work for me," I said. "You know how to find us?"

"I do," Ron said. "I'll see you later."

I called Ruby to find out if Anita was still in town.

"She is," Ruby said. "In fact, I'm bringing her to tai chi tonight."

"I just have a couple of questions I wanted to ask her," I said. "Do you think she'd mind?"

"No, I'm sure Anita would be happy to answer them."

I thanked Ruby and told her I'd see her at class.

The rest of the day was busy. Burtis brought the tables for the yard sale. A new reading club brought oatmeal cookies with walnuts and raisins. Several boxes of books were delivered.

Ron Swan showed up at five after three. He was a solid, stocky man with the build of a hockey goalie. His head was shaved smooth, which was how I saw the scar that cut across the left side of his scalp. He looked stern and a little intimidating until he smiled and his face became all warmth.

Ron checked out the alarm system from top to bottom. "My recommendation is to update what you have. With a couple of additions I think the building would be more secure and you'd be spending a lot less money than buying a whole new system, which I don't think you need anyway. You definitely do need something better on the loading dock, though."

"Harry's been saying that for years," I said.

Ron smiled. "Smart man. I should have a proposal for you

in a couple of days." He handed me a list of references. "I figured Larry said good things about me because we've known each other for years, but I thought you'd like some less biased opinions."

"Thank you," I said.

Susan came out of the stacks pushing an empty book cart just as Ron was leaving. There was a bamboo skewer and a tuning fork poked in her updo.

"What was Ron Swan doing here?" she asked.

I explained that I had asked him to look at the library's alarm system.

"He installed the alarm system at the café," Susan said. "He's a good guy and he stands behind his work."

"You're the second person to speak highly of Ron and his company," I said.

"I'm guessing the first one was Larry."

I nodded.

"He recommended Ron to Eric. If the board decides to use his company I think you'll be happy." She smiled. "And now segueing from good guy to bad guy, have you figured out Will Redfern's connection to the theft of the paintings yet?"

"Maybe," I hedged.

"Good to hear," Susan said. She moved closer to me. "I didn't like Bridget suggesting the police weren't working hard on Will's murder. Marcus wouldn't do that. Keep going, Kathleen, someone needs to figure this out."

At the end of the day I headed home to the boys. Hercules was in the porch as usual. Owen was sitting in the wing chair in the living room.

"That is a people chair, not a cat chair," I told him.

He looked around at the chair and seemed to act surprised. Then he lay down again.

I folded my arms and glared at him. "You could be replaced with a nice bowl of goldfish," I said.

He stretched and rolled over on his back. There was a gleam of triumph in his golden eyes. My bluff had just been called by a cat.

I ate the last of the spaghetti sauce with fusilli for supper, and since the rain was over and the sky was clear, I decided to walk to tai chi. Marcus was picking me up afterward. "He's bringing Micah," I announced to the empty kitchen. After a moment I heard a meow from the basement and another one from the porch. Neither sounded like an objection.

All three cats got along very well—much better than I'd anticipated. I thought maybe it was because they were all Wisteria Hill cats. A couple of times all three of them had put their heads together, seemingly communicating without making a sound.

"They could be planning some come kind of coup," Marcus had jokingly said.

"That is not as far-fetched as it sounds," I'd replied, "assuming they can get Fifi and possibly Boris to do most of the heavy lifting."

Rebecca was changing her shoes when I got to tai chi.

"I didn't get to talk to you last class," I said. "The shower was so much fun. Thank you. I know you helped Roma and Maggie."

Rebecca smiled. "It was my pleasure. I like seeing you and Marcus get your happily ever after."

I sat down next to her and pulled my own shoes out of my bag.

"I don't mean to be a nosy busybody," she said. "But have the two of you decided where you're going to live once you're married?"

I shook my head. "Not exactly, but as soon as we do, I'll let Everett know."

Rebecca waved away my words. "He isn't in any hurry. Selfishly, I would hate to lose you and Owen and Hercules."

Suddenly there was a huge lump in the back of my throat, and I was afraid I might start to cry. "You're the best neighbor I've ever had," I managed to choke out.

Rebecca hugged me, patting my back with one hand. "Things will work out the way they're supposed to, my dear," she said.

I changed my shoes and went inside. Ruby and Anita were with Maggie. I walked over to say hello.

Anita smiled. "I just heard you're getting married. Congratulations!"

"Thank you," I said.

"Is the wedding here in Mayville Heights?"

I nodded. "It is." I explained about Wisteria Hill and the old carriage house just as Roma joined us.

Ruby did the introductions.

"Roma's husband, Eddie, built a new home for the feral cats," I told Anita. I explained how Smokey had taken to Eddie. Smokey was the oldest cat in the feral cat colony. He had gotten his name from his smoke-gray fur.

"Eddie likes talking to Smokey," Roma said. "They seem to have the same opinion on a lot of things, especially meat substitutes, wild card teams and which way the toilet paper goes on the roll. Trust me, do not get into a debate on that last one with either of them."

"Cats are very good judges of character," Anita said with a smile. She turned to me. "I saw the calendars Ruby did with your cats. They're fantastic."

"That's because Ruby is an excellent photographer," I said.

"Owen and Hercules were great subjects to photograph," Ruby said with a smile. "A lot easier than some people I've worked with to take photos of."

"I'm leaving tomorrow afternoon," Anita said, "and I don't want to impose, but is there any chance I could stop by to see them?"

"I don't go into work until lunchtime tomorrow," I said. "You could stop by sometime in the morning."

"I'd be happy to drive you," Ruby offered. "I love to see the furballs."

"Thank you so much," Anita said. She shook her head. "I'm sorry. I've been talking way too much. Ruby said there were a couple of things you wanted to ask me."

"I was wondering what you could tell me about Jameson Quilleran."

"Jamie was good to work with. He'd been hired by the museum to flesh out the history of the various paintings and write the descriptions for the exhibit catalogue and for the information cards that went with each painting. Everything he wrote was factual, but he liked to weave all the little details into a story of sorts. And he was very good at it." She smiled. "He liked to have a good time as far as his private life was concerned but he was meticulous about his work and his research."

She brushed a bit of lint off the front of her shirt. "I'm guessing you've heard that Jamie clashed with Robert Hamilton a couple of times and you've also probably heard he had a bit of a temper."

I was surprised to hear about conflict with Hamilton, but I didn't want Anita to know that. She might be more circumspect about what she said if she did. "Do you have any idea why they didn't get along?" I asked.

"Jamie took issue with some of the backstory for a couple of the paintings. There were documents missing or incomplete and in one case he believed the details about one of the paintings being part of an exhibition in Chicago were a complete fabrication. I know how he felt because I had some issues with the provenance. The problem was that Jamie wasn't exactly . . .

diplomatic. He kept using the word 'sketchy' and Mr. Hamilton took offense." She gave a wry smile. "Jamie is good at what he does, very good, and if Mr. Hamilton had him fired it would have delayed the exhibit. So he put up with Jamie, but he was—is—the kind of man who wants what he wants. There was no way they were going to get along. The second argument happened because Jamie said art should be in public collections, not private ones. Since Mr. Hamilton had a large private collection of paintings and sculptures, he took offense. He didn't see that he had an obligation to share his artwork."

"I know Mr. Quilleran went to a court-ordered anger management class," I said.

Anita nodded. "That had nothing to do with Mr. Hamilton. The incident that led to that happened just before the robbery. Not to excuse Jamie losing his cool, but we were all under the gun at that point. Everyone wanted the exhibit to go well." She shrugged. "I'm not sure if he learned much about not letting his anger get out of control, but he did say it was good to be around people who understood what it was like to feel strongly about things."

I glanced at Maggie. It was almost time for class to start.

"If you do figure out how the painting ended up at your library, will you let me know, please?" Anita asked.

"I will," I said.

If only I could figure that out.

chapter 11

ircle, everyone," Maggie called, clapping her hands.

Anita turned out to be very good at the form. She was fluid and smooth in her movements and I felt a small twinge of jealousy when I watched her Cloud Hands.

Marcus picked me up after class. Micah was waiting on the front seat of his SUV. She climbed onto my lap and I stroked her soft fur.

As we started up the hill Marcus shot me a sideways glance and said, "You were right."

"About what?" I asked.

"Will Redfern and Jameson Quilleran *were* in the same

anger management class. The more I thought about what you'd said, the more sense it made. So I did a little digging."

"Yes!" I exclaimed with a little fist pump.

Marcus smiled. "You can say, 'I told you so.'"

I smiled back at him. "I don't have to. It's implied in the fist pump."

Micah meowed loudly in agreement.

"The link between the two men is tenuous, but now I do think it's possible Will had a connection to the theft of those paintings or maybe just to the one that ended up at the library. I just don't know what it is."

"I talked to Anita Marler," I said. "She came to class. Jameson Quilleran and Robert Hamilton did not get along and it seems Quilleran didn't think much of private art collections. It gives him a possible motive for the theft."

"Possible, yes," Marcus said. "But you have to admit it's a bit of a leap from meeting someone in an anger management class to saying, 'Hey, want to rob a rich guy with me?' And you know Will's alibi is rock-solid."

"Maybe Jameson Quilleran's isn't," I said. "Sometimes alibis can be a bit stretchy."

Owen was waiting in the kitchen for us. He meowed at Micah, who meowed back at him. He headed for the living room and she followed.

"Stay off that chair," I called after them.

"The guys are taking me camping the weekend after next for a bachelor weekend," Marcus said as he hung up his jacket.

"Is that code for sitting in the woods and drinking beer for two days?" I asked.

He grinned. "No. It's code for going rock climbing."

I gave him a look. "Rock climbing. Really?"

He nodded. "It's something I've always wanted to try."

I stretched up to kiss him. "Please try not to come back in a full body cast."

Marcus left very early the next morning. I was still sitting at the table, slightly bleary-eyed, clutching my coffee.

Micah refused to move from her spot on my lap. "I'll drop her off at your place on my way to work," I said.

"Mrrr," she said. That sounded like a "Fine by me."

Since I was up so early I sent an email to Jameson Quilleran explaining who I was and asking if we could talk. There was a six-hour difference between our two time zones and I knew it was a long shot that he'd even respond.

"Merow," Micah said as I hit send on the e-mail.

"Exactly," I said. "No guts, no glory."

Five minutes later I got a response in which Quilleran included his number and an invitation to video call him right now.

Jameson Quilleran was even better looking than in the photographs I'd seen. He had a thick head of dark hair steaked with gray and striking blue eyes. There were fine lines around his eyes, which were the only giveaway to his age. His smile was warm and he had an easygoing manner. I could see how people would readily be charmed by him.

"Call me Jamie," he said in his lovely British accent. "May I call you Kathleen?"

"Please," I said. I explained about Will and the missing painting turning up in the library.

"Robert Hamilton will be in your debt," he said, "which is not a bad thing. I've already talked to the police, what can I do for you?"

"Do you have any idea how that painting ended up in my library?" I asked.

He laughed. "Your guess is as good as mine." He raised an eyebrow. "In case you're curious, I didn't stash it there, although I have been in the building a number of times."

"You have?" I said.

"I have what you might call a complicated family," he said. "My father is British but my mother is actually American. Both of them have been married more than once. The woman I consider to be my grandmother is actually my aunt. She lives in a retirement community between Red Wing and Mayville Heights. I've returned her library books several times when I've been visiting. It's a beautiful building. A Carnegie library if I'm not mistaken."

"That's right," I said. "The building was restored for its centennial several years ago. And for the record, I didn't think you had hidden the painting. I know you have an alibi for the time of the robbery."

He shrugged. "Ah, but that didn't stop people from suspecting me for quite a while, including the mighty Mr. Hamilton himself."

He gave me that boyish smile once again and I noticed how he positioned his head so he didn't have a double chin on camera.

Micah suddenly jumped up onto my lap. She settled herself so she could see the screen. "Hello, puss," Jamie said.

"Merow," Micah replied.

Jamie laughed and looked at me. "He or she?"

"She," I said. "Micah."

"So you're a cat person?" he asked.

I nodded.

"Me as well. I have two. Fred and Ginger." He smiled. "But I'm getting off topic. Is there anything else you wanted to know?"

"Did you know Will Redfern?"

He ran a hand through his hair. "Did I know Will Redfern? The police asked that same question. He may have been in my anger management class—I don't remember. Then again, I don't really remember anyone from that class. I was deeply embarrassed and I just wanted to get it done. I showed up, sat at the front and took notes. I did not socialize."

He was lying. His eyes didn't meet mine, he had repeated my question and his responses seemed very practiced.

"I think it's just a very odd coincidence that the painting ended up at your library and Mr. Redfern and I seem to have been in the same class. Coincidences do happen." He gave me that smile again. "You know, sometimes a cigar is just a cigar."

But not as often as he wanted me to think.

"Thank you for talking to me," I said.

"It was my pleasure," he said. "If you ever figure out how the painting ended up in the library, please let me know." Interesting that Anita had said the same thing. It was the question everyone wanted answered.

"I will," I said, and we ended the call.

I got another cup of coffee and took it outside. Micah followed. I sat on one of the Adirondack chairs and Micah jumped up onto the other. I looked around and sighed. "I'm going to miss this place," I said, "but it makes the most sense for us all to live in Marcus's house. I'm going to tell him that the boys and I will be moving in." I felt sad but I was also relieved to have made the choice.

After a few minutes we went back inside. Owen poked his head around the basement door. Somehow one ear was turned half inside out and there was a clump of dryer lint on his head. At the same time Hercules appeared in the living room doorway. He was a bit shame-faced, dragging one of my scarves behind him, snagged on his claws.

Micah looked at both of them and then at me. She meowed softly.

I nodded. "I know," I said.

Since Owen was closer I fixed his ear and grabbed the lint off his head first. Then I disentangled the scarf from Herc's paw.

"Stay out of my dresser drawer," I said. If I didn't push it all the way in he could always manage to get a paw on an edge and pull it partly open. I looked back over my shoulder. "And stop hiding catnip frogs and chickens behind the dryer," I told Owen. He suddenly became engrossed in washing his right paw.

I got to my feet. "Boys," I said softly to Micah.

I got breakfast for the cats and then for myself. I tossed in a load of laundry, made a grocery list and deep-cleaned the bathroom.

"We have visitors coming," I told all three cats when I came down for another cup of coffee.

Owen began to wash his face. Hercules headed for the porch. I knew he'd keep watch out the window. Micah cocked her head to one side and looked at me. I explained who was coming. "Please don't show off your skills while they're here."

Micah looked at me and then vanished. I sighed and looked up at the ceiling for a moment. "Like that," I said. A moment later she reappeared. She wandered into the living room. I had a feeling she was laughing at me.

Ruby and Anita arrived right on time. Anita was charmed by all three cats, who were on their best behavior.

"I explained about touching Owen and Hercules," Ruby said.

"You're welcome to pet Micah," I said. "Roma thinks she

may have been someone's pet who was abandoned, but Owen and Hercules were almost certainly feral from birth and they don't like being touched by anyone other than me."

That wasn't totally true. Both Owen and Hercules would happily sit on Harrison's lap but only his and that was too complicated to explain.

Anita was petting Micah, who loved the attention. "What happens if someone does touch the other two?" she asked.

Ruby laughed. "In a word, claws."

I nodded.

Anita smiled at the boys. "You're entitled to body autonomy just like anyone else."

Owen gave an enthusiastic meow as though he'd understood what she'd said. I suspected he did. Or he just liked the attention.

As I walked Ruby and Anita to Ruby's car, Fifi peeked at us from the edge of the driveway. Anita was captivated. "What a beautiful animal," she said.

"That's Fifi," I said. "He's a little timid."

She looked from the dog to me. "He?"

I nodded. Then I patted my leg. "C'mon, boy," I called. After a bit of hesitation, over he came.

Anita set her bag down, leaned over and offered her hand. Fifi sniffed it and looked up at me a bit uncertainly.

"It's all right," I said. He stayed by my side but he did let Anita scratch the top of his head. After a minute or so he barked once and headed home.

"He liked you," I said to Anita. "Fifi isn't usually that friendly with new people."

She straightened up, brushing a bit of dirt off her pants. "You have some wonderful animal friends in your life," she said.

I smiled. "You're right. I do." Out of the corner of my eye I could see what looked to be a piece of black plastic seemingly suspended in the air headed for the backyard. *Oh, Owen, what did you do?* I thought. I said good-bye to Anita and Ruby and waved as they drove off. Then I scurried back to the house.

The piece of plastic was suspended several inches above the top step of the back stoop. "Owen, what have you done?" I said.

I heard a low "mrrr" at my feet and looked down to see Owen sitting there. I felt that bottom-dropping-out-of-your-stomach sensation that comes when the roller coaster crests a hill, and then Micah winked into appearance on the stoop, the piece of plastic held delicately in her mouth.

I held out my hand and she dropped it onto my palm. I sank onto the step below the cat. Owen was glaring at me. "I'm sorry," I said. "I jumped to a conclusion. I shouldn't have misjudged you."

He turned his head and looked the other way, chin up, body rigid. Owen could be more dramatic than some people.

I turned my attention to Micah. I held up the piece of plastic. "Where did you get this?" I said.

The cat's response was to lean over and nudge it with her nose. I took a closer look and realized it wasn't a piece of plastic

I was holding. It was a plastic-coated wire with a metal alligator clip at one end. I stared at it for a long moment.

Micah seemed to have gotten bored and had started to wash her face. Owen forgot he was giving me the silent treatment, put his paws on the edge of the step and peered at the wire and clip.

I realized there was only one place Micah could have gotten this—Anita's bag. She'd set it down in the driveway to pay attention to Fifi. I also knew exactly where I'd seen a piece of wire with a clip just like it—on the device that had been used to circumvent the alarm system at the library.

"I need to talk to Marcus," I said. I headed inside, followed by both cats.

I kicked off my shoes and my cell phone rang. I picked it up off the table.

It was Alphonse Dupont, the security guard I'd been trying to contact.

"Ms. Paulson, I apologize for not calling back sooner. I've been on a fishing trip. I read about the painting being found in the library and I'm guessing that's why you called."

"Thank you for returning my call," I said. "I know that the police cleared you as a suspect in the robbery. I just want to know what happened that night. Will Redfern—the man whose body was found at the library—and I have a history. I'm trying to figure out if he could have been involved somehow."

"I know Redfern attacked you and went to jail for it," Alphonse said. "It was in the newspaper story I read."

I took a deep breath and let it out slowly. "I would like to give Will the benefit of the doubt in this case."

"But you're not sure that you should."

"Exactly," I said.

"I'm happy to tell you what I told the police," Alphonse said. "I didn't see or hear anything the night those paintings were taken." There was no hesitation in his voice. "Despite what happened, Terry Long—the other guard—and I were treated well by Mr. Hamilton. He even paid the vet bill for Rex's surgery about a month or so later."

"Rex?" I said.

"Yeah, Terry's dog. He was a big German shepherd. He was trained for security work. Rex was a sweetie, gentle and friendly when he wasn't working, but when his harness went on he was all business. Nobody with any sense would have messed with that dog."

Both Owen and Micah were watching me intently. "So what do you think happened?"

"I always thought it was the company that installed the new security system at the house. I think they were lax with the alarm codes. The thieves knew what they were after. They were in and out in minutes. The only reason me and Terry knew anything happened was because the alarm company noticed two power interruptions close together and called to see if everything was all right."

"Power interruptions?" I said. "You mean the power was off when the paintings were stolen?"

"No, no," Alphonse said, "nothin' like that. There were just a couple of power surges. I mean just seconds."

"Did you ever meet Jameson Quilleran?"

He laughed. "The English guy. Talk about tightly wound. He and Mr. Hamilton had a couple of set-tos but they seemed to work it out. At least, he didn't get fired. Anyway, I didn't have much to do with him. The man wasn't the type to associate with the help, if you know what I mean."

I smiled. "Yes, I do. What about Anita Marler?"

"She was a bit intense with all the animal rights stuff she was involved in but I can't really fault her for that. Anyone who would hurt an animal is pretty low, and if you'll hurt an animal you probably won't have many qualms about hurting a person. She made chocolate chip cookies a few times and brought some for me and Terry and she actually made dog biscuits for Rex."

My mind was racing all over the place. "Is there anything else you wanna know?" he asked.

"Did Rex bark?" I said.

"You mean the night of the robbery?"

"Yes."

"No, he didn't. Somehow the thief or thieves got in and out without the dog knowing, and he spent a lot of the time prowling the property off leash."

"Thank you for talking to me, Mr. Dupont," I said.

"I'm not sure I helped," he said.

"You helped more than you know. I appreciate it."

We ended the call and I folded both arms over the top of my head. I was overwhelmed by all the things I had learned in the last half hour. The wire and clip that Micah had "found" looked like it could be part of the same kind of device Will had used to get past the alarm system at the library. One other thing, however, stuck out.

I dropped my arms to see a couple of furry faces looking at me. "I think Anita Marler might be the thief," I said.

chapter 12

The dog didn't bark," I said.

They both looked blankly at me. Neither one of them seemed to see the significance of that piece of information.

"The security guard's dog didn't bark at the thief. Why? Because the dog knew the person. It's the only thing that makes sense."

Micah and Owen exchanged a look.

"Anita made dog treats."

Owen looked over at the cats' treat cupboard.

"Owen, try to focus," I said. He made a low grumble of annoyance.

"Anita made friends with the dog—Rex—which makes sense because she loves animals, but it also meant the dog knew her well enough that he didn't bark when he saw her. Alphonse said she made cookies for him and the other guard. I bet she spent time talking to them as well, finding out about their routine."

I leaned against the counter, trying to put the pieces together in some sort of pattern that made sense. I felt like I was putting together the edges of a puzzle. "Anita worked for months getting the exhibit together, checking all the backgrounds of the paintings. I'm betting in the beginning she did befriend Rex because she likes animals so much, but at some point she became more calculating." I blew out a breath. "I have to call Marcus right now."

Micah meowed with enthusiasm. Owen yawned. It seemed I'd only made my case to one of them.

I expected I'd have to leave a message for Marcus but he answered on the third ring. I shared my reasoning and waited for him to find fault with my logic.

He didn't. "It makes sense," he said slowly. "And you were right about the connection between Will and Jameson Quilleran. I think you're right about this, too." He paused. "I need to check out a couple of things. I'll call you later." He ended the call before I even had a chance to say good-bye.

I looked down at Micah. Owen had disappeared. Literally or figuratively, I wasn't sure. "He agreed with me," I said.

She wrinkled her whiskers at me.

I nodded. "I know. I wasn't expecting that, either."

Marcus called me back just as I was about to leave for the library. "I only have a minute," he said. "I did a little more checking into Anita's alibi, based on the idea that she was involved in the break-in, at least in part. It wasn't quite as good as it first seemed. Her animal activist friends had a reason to cover for her. She'd promised money for their cause. We're going to bring her in for questioning and I'm pretty sure she'll be arrested. I'm not convinced she was working alone, though."

"What about Will's murder?" I asked.

Marcus exhaled loudly. "That she's not responsible for."

I wasn't surprised. I didn't see how someone who cared so much for dogs and cats could have hurt anyone.

"Her alibi for that is airtight."

"You're certain? Better than your father and Burtis's?"

I was surprised to hear him laugh. "Actually, it is. Her alibi for the time of Will's murder comes from a priest and two nuns."

"Seriously? It sounds too good to be true."

"It's not. Anita was at a fund-raiser for an animal shelter. They were with her all evening."

I told Marcus I'd drop by the police station on my way to work with the piece of wire Micah had "found," and we said good-bye.

Word about Anita Marler's arrest spread quickly. Ruby came into the library late in the afternoon with more boxes of things for the yard sale. "I don't know what to say," she said, shaking her head. "I can't believe Anita was involved in that robbery. I'm so sorry I recommended her."

"You had no way of knowing," I said. "For the past six years she had basically gotten away with it."

"You don't think she had anything to do with what happened to . . . Will, do you?" Ruby asked.

I shook my head. "I have it on good authority that she didn't."

Ruby gave a sigh of relief.

I was glad Anita Marler hadn't killed Will, but I still didn't know who had.

Saturday morning I went out to Ella's to try on my dress. To my surprise Roma and Maggie were waiting for me in Ella's living room. "What are you two doing here?" I asked.

"Ella let us change our appointment," Roma said. "We wanted to see you in your dress. Is that all right?"

I hugged them both. "Yes, it's all right."

"Sarah tried on her dress when she was here for your shower," Ella said. "It fit perfectly. I just have to finish the hem on Hannah's."

Roma and Maggie went to change first. They came out together and I choked up. "You look so . . . so beautiful," I said. I clasped both of my hands to my chest. The dresses were identical to the one I'd seen Hannah in, with the same neckline, delicate sleeves and flowing skirt. Maggie and Roma had different coloring and different body types, but the soft shade of blue-green flattered both of them, just as it had Hannah.

Maggie waved one hand in the air. "Don't make me cry."

"More importantly, don't wrinkle the merchandise," Ella said.

I grabbed one of Maggie's hands and one of Roma's and gave them each a squeeze instead.

"They look even better than the sketches," I said to Ella.

She smiled. "I'm so glad you like them." She pinned the hems of both dresses, making both Maggie and Roma turn in slow circles. Finally she stepped back and nodded.

Then it was my turn to try on my dress. "It's going to be a little long, even with your shoes," Ella warned. "And I'm probably going to have to adjust the waist, so don't panic."

The dress was everything I had imagined for a wedding gown. Mom had come for a long weekend and we'd spent an afternoon with Ella, eating Rebecca's oatmeal cookies while Ella sketched out our ideas. In the end I had settled on a simple, elegant dress. It had a fitted bodice overlaid with lace, a bateau neckline and tiny buttons up the back. The straight-cut skirt gave me room to move.

Ella fastened the tiny pearl and rhinestone buttons and adjusted the sleeves. "I'll give you a minute," she said.

I picked up my phone and called my mother. She answered on the first ring. "Hello, Katydid," she said.

I smiled, even as I felt the prickle of tears. "Ready to see the dress?" I asked.

She smiled and nodded. "I already know you're going to be beautiful."

I stretched out my arm so she could see the whole dress. Then I brought the phone closer so I could see her face. "Do you like it?"

"The day you were born I thought you were the most beautiful thing I had ever seen and you still are," she said. "And don't tell your brother and sister I said that."

I laughed and tried to swallow down the lump of emotion in my chest at the same time. A sound came out like a cross between a hiccup and a burp. "I love you," I managed to say.

She blew me a kiss. "I love you, too, Katydid."

I said good-bye, put my phone away and took one last look at myself in the full-length mirror. Then I went out to join Maggie and Roma.

Maggie put a hand on her chest. "Oh wow," she said softly.

Roma just smiled and nodded her head.

"What do you think?" Ella asked.

"I think it's perfect," I said. "I don't know how to thank you."

She smiled. "That's easy. Love that guy of yours and be happy." She made a twirling gesture with one finger. "Now turn around so I can see the whole dress."

I turned in a slow circle. Ella frowned at one sleeve and took in a tiny pinch of fabric at my waist.

Maggie came up behind me. "Those buttons are beautiful," she said to Ella.

Ella nodded. "The moment I saw them I knew they would be perfect for Kathleen's dress. I found them in a little antique shop in Red Wing. They're at least fifty years old. Probably older."

Maggie leaned her head against mine for a moment. "You look beautiful," she said. Roma joined us.

Ella moved her finger between the two of them. "Remember what I told you. Don't wrinkle the merchandise."

Maggie waited until Ella turned to reach for her pins and gave my shoulders a squeeze. Roma settled for taking both of my hands in hers. "We love you," she said.

"And I love you," I said. "I wouldn't want to get married without the two of you beside me." I looked down at the dress and up at them again. "This is real. I'm getting married."

"Not if you don't hold still so I can put some pins in the waist and the hem of this dress you're not," Ella said. She looked at Maggie and Roma. "Stop distracting my bride and go take those dresses off before they get any more wrinkled." She pointed in the direction of the spare room that doubled as a dressing room.

"We're going," Maggie said. She grinned at me over her shoulder. Roma followed, humming "Here Comes the Bride" just under her breath.

"Just be careful of the pins when you take the dresses off," Ella called after them as they went to change.

Marcus picked me up for Duncan's ball game right after lunch. "It seems Anita Marler has decided there is no honor among thieves."

"What do you mean?" I asked.

"You know that I thought she didn't steal those paintings by herself."

I nodded.

"And I was right. She and Jameson Quilleran were in it together. Anita's job was to get him into the building—she did distract the dog and get the device to bypass the alarm from one of her animal activist friends. He took the paintings and fenced them."

"What was their motive?" I asked.

"She wanted the money for her animal rescue work. He just wanted the money, period."

"So at least in his case, everything that Quilleran had said about art being available to everybody and not in private collections was just meaningless rhetoric."

Marcus nodded. "It looks that way."

"So what's going to happen to him?"

"Mr. Quilleran has already been arrested by the police in London. He'll be extradited back here eventually. He has dual citizenship."

"Is it possible that he's the one who killed Will?" I asked.

"It doesn't look like it," Marcus said. "We can't find any record of him leaving London around the time of Will's murder. I'm hoping once I can talk to the guy I can get more answers."

The kids were just arriving when we got to the ball field. I saw Rebecca with Duncan and Riley. Duncan's face lit up and he ran over to me. "You came," he said.

"Of course I came," I said. "I can't wait to see you play."

"You can sit with Riley and Rebecca." He leaned in closer and lowered his voice. "Sometimes Rebecca has cookies in her purse."

"What kind of cookies?" I asked.

He thought for a moment. "The last time was chocolate chip."

"My favorite."

He smiled. "Mine too." He glanced over his shoulder at the dugout. "I have to go warm up. Don't forget after the game I'm giving you a throwing lesson."

"I didn't forget," I said. "Good luck."

He smiled and ran off to join the other kids.

Rebecca waved at me and patted a space on the bleachers between her and Riley. I went to join them. "What are you doing here?" I said to Rebecca.

"Lita had a wedding to go to so I get to watch Duncan play," she said. "It's a second cousin and a third wedding." She frowned. "Or maybe it's the other way around."

"What are *you* doing here?" Riley said.

I smiled at her. "I was invited."

"You mean by the squirt." She tipped her head toward Duncan and Marcus, who were warming up near the dugout.

"I mean by the pitcher," I said, giving her a haughty look.

She laughed and shook her head.

I nudged her with my shoulder. "So what's new with you?" I asked.

She shrugged. "Not much. Well, I'm sorta going to math camp this summer 'cause I kinda won a bursary." That was typical Riley, downplaying her accomplishments.

"That's wonderful!" I exclaimed. Without thinking about it I threw my arms around her. I noticed she didn't pull away.

Rebecca leaned forward. "It is wonderful news, Riley. I'm proud of you."

"It's not that big a deal," Riley said in her usual self-deprecating way. "They give a bunch of bursaries for kids like me."

"You mean smart kids?" I said.

She made a face at me. "I mean kids without any parents."

"Doesn't matter," I said. "It's math camp. I'm a little jealous."

"You never went to one?" she said.

"I never went to any kind of camp."

She looked surprised. "How come?"

"You know my parents are actors, right?"

She nodded.

"Well, when I was a kid they were always doing some kind of summer theater, and they took me with them."

"My goodness, what did you do with yourself?" Rebecca asked.

"Mostly hung around with the backstage crew, played a lot of road hockey and pinball and read a lot of books."

"I always pictured you being the kind of kid who rode around on your bike with your dog and went to camp and roasted marshmallows and stuff," Riley said.

I shook my head. "I never had a bike," I said. "Well, technically I had one for two days but it got stolen. No dog because we were away so much. Owen and Hercules are the first pets I ever had. And like I said, I didn't go to camp." I smiled. "But I did learn how to make s'mores on a hot plate."

Riley stared at me. "But I always thought you had a perfect childhood."

"Nobody has a perfect childhood," I said. "I was happy— most of the time. I had parents who loved me. I had friends. I got really good at playing pinball. I learned how to cook. I learned how to fix a toilet with dental floss." I raised one eyebrow. "All useful life skills, by the way."

"Next time I need a plumber I'm calling you first," Rebecca said.

I grinned. "As long as you have dental floss, I'm your woman. You can pay me in cookies."

Susan came scrambling up the bleachers then and dropped onto a spot in front of Rebecca. Her topknot was listing a little to the right, anchored today with a bamboo fork and a glass straw.

"Hey, guys," she said, smiling up at us.

"Are the boys playing?" I asked.

She nodded. "Harry recruited them."

The kids were taking the field and we all turned our attention in that direction. Duncan pitched well and got a hit in the third inning. All three of us cheered when the next batter brought him home. I saw him look in our direction, smiling with pride, and I resolved I was going to come to every game he had.

It was halfway through the fourth inning when I noticed Gerald Hollister standing off to one side. I caught Rebecca's eye and tipped my head in Gerald's direction. She pressed her lips together and gave her head a little shake.

An inning later he was standing next to the bleachers. "Riley, girl, how are you?" he said.

Both of Riley's hands tightened into fists. "None of your damn business, old man," she said.

"I'm your grandfather. Show some respect," he retorted.

"Respect is something you earn. You haven't earned mine."

I put my arm around her shoulders. I could feel the tension in her body like tightly coiled cables under her skin. I looked at Gerald. His eyes were cold and angry. "Riley doesn't want to talk to you," I said. "You should leave."

"My family is none of your business, Ms. Paulson," he said. His expression turned mocking. "I heard about Will Redfern's body at your library. My, my, dead bodies do seem to keep turning up around you."

Riley lunged toward him but I managed to grab her before she reached him. She was breathing hard and shaking. "Don't give him the satisfaction," I murmured.

Rebecca had already turned to Gerald. She was talking to him in a low, steady voice, gesturing with one hand. Rebecca was generally able to reason with the man. Gerald had a soft spot for her. It made me nervous.

I kept both arms tightly around Riley. I understood her impulse to go after her grandfather. I was feeling the same thing. "I hate him," she said through clenched teeth.

Finally, Gerald moved away and Rebecca turned to us. "Are you both all right?" she asked. There were tight lines around her eyes and mouth.

"I'm fine," I said.

Riley nodded, her body still rigid with anger.

"Riley, has your grandfather approached you before today?" Rebecca asked.

"Twice," she said.

"Has he tried to talk to Duncan?"

"If he goes near Duncan I'll hurt him."

I had no doubt at all that she would.

"I understand the impulse," Rebecca said, "but that would play right into your grandfather's hands. If he contacts you again or if he comes anywhere near Duncan I want you to tell Lita. Do you understand? Or call me or Kathleen."

"I can take care of myself and Duncan." I'd heard that stubborn edge in her voice before.

I leaned forward so I was in her line of sight. "We know that. Gerald is trying to make trouble. Don't make it easier for him." She wouldn't look me in the eye but she hadn't made any move to pull away from me, either. "Please, Riley," I said softly.

She finally looked at me. "All right," she said.

I let go of her and she tried to bolt down the bleachers but I had guessed she'd try to do that and I had a handful of her sweater. I pulled her down on the seat beside me.

"He's evil, Kathleen," she said. "He's evil and I hate him."

"I know that," I said. "And so does he. He will use that against you. Keep your cool. I know how hard it is but you need to do it."

Both of Riley's hands were pulled into tight fists and she was breathing hard. "You know what he did? He put a gate at the bottom of the driveway. No one can get to the house unless he comes and lets them in. And if you touch it, you get a shock."

Gerald had always been a bit paranoid, not really surprising for someone who had little respect for the law, so I wasn't surprised. "I'll tell Marcus, and you need to stay away from your grandfather and the house."

After a moment she nodded. She stared out at the field. Rebecca was watching us, concern knotting her forehead, but she didn't say anything.

"You're pretty fast," Riley finally said. She still wasn't looking at me.

I shrugged. "It's all that pinball. I have lightning reflexes."

The tiniest twitch of a smile tugged at her lips. "I bet I could beat you," she said.

"There's only one way to find out."

She finally did look at me then. "Your brain has already passed its reaction-time peak by more than ten years. It's slowing down every day that goes by. My brain is still getting faster and better."

I pointed one finger at her. "You are going down, girl," I said.

She laughed. "Yeah, you keep telling yourself that, old lady." She leaned against me for a moment then straightened up and pointed at the field. "Duncan's up," she said.

Rebecca and Riley turned their attention to the game.

I felt the hairs rise on the back of my neck. Someone was watching me. I knew who it had to be. Out of the corner of my eye I could see Gerald looking in this direction. I turned my head to look at him, my gaze defiant. After a minute he turned away. I felt a childish rush of satisfaction about that.

At the midpoint of the inning I leaned forward and tapped Susan on the shoulder. She turned to look at me. "Thanks for working for me this morning," I said.

"Oh, you're welcome," she said. "How did the fitting go?"

"The dress is beautiful. It's everything I wanted but couldn't seem to put into words."

Susan smiled. "Ella is very talented." Susan and Ella had recently discovered they were related and had already formed a tight bond.

Susan glanced at the field and then turned her attention back to me. "I don't mean to be nosy, but someone looked at the three paintings you bought from the library sale, right?"

"You mean the sunflower and the two watercolors of the fishing villages in Spain? No. Those paintings came from a box that was donated by Rebecca."

Susan shook her head. "No, they didn't. They were in a box in the basement along with a bunch of other pieces of artwork."

"Uh, no. You're wrong," I said. "I remember taking them out of a box. It had 'Library Book Sale' written on the side in red marker in Rebecca's handwriting."

"I know. But the three paintings you bought came from the library's basement. I have photos somewhere of the boxes. The one they were in was damp and it fell apart. I stuck everything in the box from Rebecca. I thought you knew."

"I didn't." And it didn't matter. All of the paintings that were stolen from Robert Hamilton had been accounted for now that the watercolor had been found.

Susan looked over at the game again. "For all we know maybe the sunflower is actually a Van Gogh."

"I don't think so," I said. "Van Gogh painted his sunflowers in oil and my painting is egg tempera."

She made a face. "Rats! I was having fantasies of finding another painting that was worth a lot of money."

I smiled. "Sorry to disappoint you."

Duncan came up to bat then and that was the end of the

conversation. He hit a double and a run scored. We all cheered wildly. I glanced around for Gerald but there was no sign of him.

In the end, Duncan's team won the game by three runs. He ran over to us and Riley smiled at him. "Good job, squirt," she said.

Rebecca opened her purse and gave him a bag of cookies. They were chocolate chip. "Thank you," he said. "I'm gonna go share them with the guys." He raced back to the dugout.

I looked at Rebecca. "You had that bag of cookies in your purse for the whole game while I was sitting next to you?" I said. "And they're chocolate chip, my favorite."

"Yes, I did," she said. "I can't believe you would even think about taking cookies belonging to a child." She gave me a mock frown but the twinkle in her blue eyes told me she wasn't really annoyed at me.

"I wouldn't have taken all of them," I said. I held up a finger. "Just one. Two maximum."

"Duncan and his friends earned those cookies," Rebecca said firmly. Then she smiled. "I'll bring you some after supper."

Duncan came back over with his glove and a ball. We moved over to a grassy spot to the left of the bleachers. "Show me how you throw," he said, all seriousness.

I backed up and tossed the ball toward him. It would have sailed right past his left shoulder if he hadn't been quick enough to snag it with his glove.

He frowned. "Okay," he said slowly. "There are some

things that maybe you could work on." He was trying so hard to be kind. "First show me how you hold the ball."

I took it from him and held it loosely in my hand, all four fingers on the top. "Like this," I said.

A frown creased his forehead. He moved my fingers farther apart. "Make fangs with your first two fingers."

"Fangs?"

"Yeah, like a snake. Or a vampire."

We spent the next twenty minutes adjusting the way I held the ball, how I threw it and where I placed my feet. The ball sailed off to the right. It went equally far off to the left. It flew way over Duncan's head. He chased after it every time and always found something positive to say to me.

"Make your other shoulder point where you want the ball to go and see it in your head going there," he said.

I blew a stray clump of hair off my face. He patted my arm. "You can do this."

I took hold of the baseball, moved my hand closer to my head, made sure my feet were set and threw. The ball sailed straight and true into Duncan's glove.

He grinned and threw his arms in the air. I did a little victory dance and then grabbed Duncan in a hug.

"I told you that you could do it," he said.

"It's because you're the best teacher," I said.

He reached into his back pocket and pulled out the plastic bag Rebecca had given him. There was one slightly crumbled cookie inside. He handed it to me. "Good job," he said.

I took a couple of deep breaths so I wouldn't cry. Then I opened the bag. I don't think any chocolate chip cookie ever tasted so good.

Rebecca agreed to let Duncan and Riley get frozen yogurt at Tubby's with Marcus and me. "Keep your eyes out," she said to me.

I knew she meant for Gerald. I nodded. "I will."

"You're coming to my next game for sure?" Duncan asked when we dropped him and Riley at Lita's house.

"Cross my heart," I said, drawing an X on the left side of my chest with one finger.

He smiled. "Practice your throwing," he said.

I promised I would.

"So when are we playing pinball?" Riley asked.

"Are you sure you want to?" I said.

She stood, feet apart, with her hands in the back pockets of her jeans, all teenage bravado. "Why not?" she said. "I'm not the one who's going to lose."

I smiled. "I'll talk to Burtis," I said. "And for the record, you *are* going to lose."

She just laughed and headed for the house.

That night Marcus and I went down to the bar in the St. James Hotel to listen to a guitar player and talk about the wedding and what was left to do. We'd finally settled on three flavors for the cake: chocolate, of course, marble and vanilla. Marcus had his suit. My dress was almost finished and we'd chosen the flowers.

After Marcus updated the list he was carrying in his wallet I told him what Riley had told me about the gate her grandfather had installed on his property and what she'd said about getting a shock from it.

"I'd heard about that gate," Marcus said, "which he has the right to have. It's his property. But I don't like the idea that it might be electrified in some way. I'll look into it."

We moved on to talk about Duncan's baseball game. "He's so serious when he plays," Marcus said. "The other kids all goof off at some point but not Duncan. He has a lot of natural ability."

"He wants to be a ball player someday," I said.

"It could happen."

"Susan reminded me of something at the game," I said. "There were three paintings that were at the library that I bought from the yard sale. I always thought Rebecca had donated them but it turns out I was wrong. Do you think there's any point in getting someone to look at them?"

"I don't see why," he said. "That watercolor was the only piece missing from Robert Hamilton's collection. And we don't even know how *it* got there. I don't think there's much chance that you're some kind of repository for stolen artwork."

"Do you think Jameson Quilleran gave that watercolor to Will to hide for him?" I asked.

Marcus tented his fingers over his glass. "I don't know.

That's a lot of trust to put in someone you've just met. And why on earth would Will have hidden it at the library?"

"Because it was only supposed to be temporary. Then he got arrested and he never had a chance to get back in the building."

"Okay, I'll concede that could have happened."

I leaned my elbows on the table and rested my chin on the back of one hand. "Do you remember the time Maggie and Roma and I followed Will and saw him kissing Ingrid?" Maggie had been convinced that Will was trying to sabotage the renovations at the library, or at least make it look like I wasn't doing my job.

"He's trying to get rid of you," she'd insisted. Will would go incommunicado on a regular basis and Maggie believed he was up to something nefarious during those times. "We need to find out where he goes when he leaves and you can't reach him." I was so frustrated with Will I'd agreed.

"I remember," Marcus said. "And it was a stupid and dangerous thing for the three of you to do."

"I might have heard that a time or two—hundred." It had turned out that Will had been having a secret relationship with my predecessor, a woman named Ingrid, who shortly after had left Mayville Heights—and Will—to audition for Cirque du Soleil.

Marcus smiled.

"Right before he headed off to meet Ingrid, Will got some tools from the storage area."

"Okay," he said slowly, probably wondering where I was going.

"I don't think Jameson Quilleran gave Will the painting. I think Will took it. He was so smug when he talked to me the day we followed him. So cocky. What if he had the painting and stashed it temporarily in the building? He had a way to get quick money and he went to get Ingrid to run off with him."

"But that didn't happen," Marcus said. "Ingrid dumped him right after that."

I was nodding before he finished speaking. "Ingrid dumped Will and he was angry. He blamed me for what happened, which is why he ended up at my house. Then he was arrested and he never got back to the library to get the painting. He wasn't allowed near me, which meant he wasn't able to get into the building. He must have thought his ship had come in when he walked in and saw the painting hanging on the wall. He wasn't going to have to hunt for it. Not only was it still in the building, it was in plain sight. Mary mentioned he had that cat-that-swallowed-the-canary look on his face. I think he believed his luck was about to change in a big way."

"Okay, let's say all this is true. We know Anita didn't kill Will unless you think Anita somehow got a priest and two nuns to lie for her. And Quilleran was in London. According to his passport he didn't leave the country and there are photos of him on his social media at a fancy party. So who killed Will?"

I sighed. "That's the part I still can't figure out."

chapter 13

I headed for the coffee shop in Red Wing the next morning to meet Reese Winters. I had no idea whether or not Robert Hamilton's former stepdaughter would be able to tell me anything useful about the theft of the man's paintings. I was convinced Will was dead because of that theft but I didn't know why.

I deliberately arrived early. I got a cup of coffee and found a small table where I could watch the door. I wanted to observe Reese before she saw me.

Reese walked in right on time and I recognized her at once. She'd described herself as being tall with white-blond hair. She caught sight of me and headed toward the table. I got to my feet. Reese smiled. "You're Kathleen," she said.

"I am," I said. "Thank you for meeting me."

She gestured over her shoulder. "I'm just going to get some coffee and I'll be right back. Do you need a refill?"

I shook my head. "Thanks. No."

I studied Reese while she got her drink. She was in her early thirties, I guessed. Her blond hair was pulled into a loose knot at the back of her head. She was wearing jeans and a white button-down shirt with a burgundy sweater over the top. She had lovely posture and I found myself sitting up straighter.

Reese returned to the table and took the chair opposite me. "I read an interview with my former stepfather. He credited you with keeping his painting safe. I hope you end up with a donation to your library out of this." She took a sip of her coffee.

It seemed clear from her tone that Reese didn't like Robert Hamilton. Which she confirmed when she said, "I'm happy to tell you about my mother but I'm not unbiased about Robert. I try not to antagonize him because I want to have a relationship with my little sister. My mother had nothing to do with the theft of the paintings, which you know because the real thieves have been arrested. But the police cleared her very quickly. And from a personal standpoint she knew how Robert felt about his possessions because she was one."

"I don't understand what you mean," I said. I wrapped both hands around my mug.

"Robert loved . . . loves . . . beautiful things and he doesn't rest until they're his. He went after my mother the same way he would after a piece of artwork he coveted. Once he got what he wanted he just wanted to show it off to his rich friends. My mother was just like a painting or a piece of sculpture to him."

Reese took out her phone, scrolled through several screens and then showed me a photo of Selena Hamilton. She was stunning with darker blond hair than her daughter and green eyes. I noticed the kindness in her gaze and the warmth of her smile.

"She was beautiful," I said.

Reese smiled. "Yes, she was and I know it sounds cliched but she was beautiful inside and out."

"Do you think there's any possibility your mother suspected that Anita Marler and Jameson Quilleran were behind the theft of the paintings?" I asked.

Reese frowned. "I don't think so. By that point all she was interested in was getting out of the marriage." She tucked a stray strand of hair behind one ear. "I'm not saying it was right for my mother to have had an affair, and no matter what people said she wasn't after any money from Robert—not even what she was guaranteed in the prenup. All she wanted was a divorce and some pieces of jewelry that had belonged to her own mother. They weren't really worth anything except for sentimental value but Robert had put them in a safe-deposit box, he claimed for safekeeping, and was stalling on both giving them back and on the divorce."

"He didn't want to end the marriage?"

"More like he was humiliated because she'd had an affair with someone he saw as a tradesman. That was Wyatt, Wyatt Hagen. He owned the landscaping company that was working at the house. Mom always believed someone who worked for Wyatt had told Robert about the two of them."

"Why would someone do that?" I asked.

Reese smiled. "Why wouldn't they? It would have been an excellent way to curry favor with my former stepfather."

She traced the rim of her mug with her index finger. "I've always believed that Mom found out something about Robert's art collection after the theft. Suddenly she got her jewelry back and the divorce went ahead and Robert made a point of publicly saying she'd had nothing to do with the theft and theirs was an amicable breakup." She gave a snort of derision. "When I asked what happened Mom said Robert found his conscience. But I know he couldn't have."

"Why not?" I said.

She picked up her mug. "Because he didn't have one."

Once I got home, I decided to make Mary's cinnamon rolls. They were as good as hers always were—in other words, delicious. I took two over to Rebecca. She cut one in half and took a bite.

"Oh those are good," she said. "I think you've perfected Mary's recipe."

Hercules had come with me and he looked up at her, head cocked to one side in his best "I'm so cute" pose.

"I'm sorry," Rebecca said to him. "Roma would hang me by my thumbs if I give you a bite."

His expression changed from cute to disgruntled.

"These really are delicious," Rebecca said, taking another bite.

"Who would have ever guessed her secret ingredient was potatoes?" I said.

Something changed in Rebecca's expression. I crossed my arms over my chest and eyed her with suspicion. "Rebecca Henderson, you knew."

Two spots of pink appeared on her cheeks. "Well . . . yes, I did," she said.

"Why didn't you tell me?' I asked. "I've been trying to duplicate that recipe for years."

"Well, first of all, Mary asked me not to and I couldn't break my promise to her."

"And second of all?"

"Every time you tried something else I got a sample. And every recipe you tried was delicious."

"Fine," I said. "I'm going to forgive you but only because I like you so much."

She smiled. "You have to admit it was fun all this time trying to figure out Mary's recipe."

I smiled back at her. "Yeah, I guess it was. I learned way more about cinnamon than I ever expected to know. And I got into a heated debate with Harrison over real versus artificial vanilla."

Rebecca laughed. "I happen to know where he stands on that subject so I know how heated that must have gotten."

I took a deep breath and let it out. There was something I wanted to say to Rebecca and I wasn't sure how she would feel.

"You look as though you have something on your mind," she said.

I nodded. "I do. I want to ask you to do something and I don't want to offend you."

"I'd be happy to do anything I could for you," she said, "and I can't imagine what you might ask that would offend me."

"Please stay away from Gerald Hollister." I held up one hand so she wouldn't start talking before I finished what I needed to say. "I don't think you're old or helpless. I just don't trust him and I don't want anything to happen to you."

"I don't trust him any more than you do," Rebecca said. "Gerald is always working an angle. And there's no need of it. He has a trade. He worked as bricklayer for years for a land-scaping company."

"What happened?" I asked.

She shrugged. "He had some kind of falling out with the owner if I remember correctly. He ended up back here doing a little of this and a little of that. Gerald is like a raccoon, except instead of collecting shiny things he collects things about people's lives that he can try to use for his own benefit. So I have a proposition for you. I'll stay away from Gerald if you do the same."

"I'd be happy to do that. You know if he comes near Riley or Duncan . . ." I didn't have to finish the sentence.

She nodded. "I feel the same."

Hercules meowed loudly.

"Looks like we all do," I said.

We talked for a few minutes about what I wanted to do with my hair for the wedding. Rebecca had been a hairdresser for years and she still cut the hair of several of her friends, including me.

"Up, I think," I said. "Or maybe over one shoulder." I laced my fingers together, rested them on my head and exhaled loudly. "The truth is, I don't know."

Rebecca patted my arm. "How about next Sunday afternoon you come over and we'll try some different things?"

I smiled gratefully. "Yes. That would help."

Hercules meowed again.

Rebecca smiled at him. "Well of course you're invited," she said. "I find a second opinion is always helpful."

I felt my chest tighten. I was really going to miss having Rebecca as my backyard neighbor.

Marcus and I spent the afternoon hiking at Wild Rose Bluff with Maggie and Brady. After that I was happy to relax on the swing on Marcus's deck with Maggie and Micah while Brady and Marcus debated the merits of the five (!) different barbeque sauces that Marcus had on hand.

Robert Hamilton showed up at five minutes to eleven on Monday with his donation to the Reading Buddies program. He didn't come alone. He also brought several reporters with him. I noticed Bridget had sent someone from the paper.

"I'm so sorry," he said. "I was trying to make this donation quietly but it seems word somehow got out."

"Isn't he afraid his nose is going to start growing on camera?" Mary said softly beside me.

Hamilton presented me with the check on the front steps of the library, thanking me for keeping the stolen painting safe for the last six years. There was no mention of Will. I swallowed down my frustration and annoyance because Reading Buddies could always use the money, but I felt used.

A large group of people had gathered. I didn't recognize about half the faces, which made me wonder how many of the people were connected to Hamilton. I spotted Gerald Hollister at the back of the crowd and prepared myself for another confrontation with him, but he simply gave me a long look and left. If he was trying to intimidate me, it wasn't working.

It was lunchtime before the whole production was over.

"I know Mr. Hamilton isn't very likable," Mary said, "but his money spends just as well as anyone else's."

I was tired when I got home. Hercules was out on the back step with Fifi instead of being inside on the bench. "What are you doing out here?" I asked.

Fifi looked at Hercules. Hercules looked at the back door and then at me.

I patted Fifi on the head. "Time for you to go home," I said. The dog looked at Hercules again.

"Merow," the cat said.

I took Fifi by the collar and tried to get him to come down the steps. He braced his feet. I couldn't move him.

"What is wrong with you two today?" I said, more than a little exasperated.

A pair of green eyes and a pair of brown eyes looked at me without blinking.

I threw up my hands, probably more dramatically than I needed to. "Fine. I'm going inside. The two of you can stay out here."

Hercules and Fifi exchanged a look. More than once I'd suspected that the cats could somehow communicate without making a sound. Given what else they could do it didn't seem that far-fetched. Now I wondered if Hercules and Fifi could do that as well. Or maybe I was just a lot more tired than I realized.

Hercules followed me into the porch. Fifi stayed where he was on the stoop. If he didn't go home in a few minutes I'd call Mike Justason. I knew he was home. I'd seen his truck in his driveway when I'd pulled into my own.

Owen was sitting in the middle of the kitchen floor as though he'd been waiting for me. He came over to me and meowed loudly. I felt the hairs rise on the back of my neck. Something was off. The chair at the end of the table closest to me was nudged a little too far to the left. It hadn't been like that when I left for work.

The basement door was closed, not slightly open, the way it had been when I'd headed for the library. I almost never shut that door completely. Owen was up and down the basement stairs several times a day.

There was dirt on the mat I was standing on, I realized. The mat that I had shaken before I left for work. And was that wood smoke I could smell?

Someone had been in my house.

It could have been Marcus, I told myself, even as I could hear my heartbeat thudding in my ears. Except I knew it hadn't been him. If Marcus had been stopping in for some reason he would have told me.

I looked at the boys. "Out," I said. "Now."

Neither one of them meowed or disappeared or refused to move. They both followed me back outside onto the steps where Fifi was waiting. The dog looked somewhat uncertainly at Owen, but he didn't move.

Was it possible that Hercules and Fifi had known someone had been in the house? Was that why they had been acting so odd?

"We're going to wait by the truck," I said.

Hercules led the way. Owen gave Fifi a wide berth and followed his brother. I followed both of them. Fifi stayed right beside me. I was happy to have him with us. I had no illusions that he would go after someone if there was anyone still inside—which I didn't think there was—but he looked and sounded intimidating and that was enough for now.

Owen and Hercules jumped up onto the hood of the truck. I leaned against the driver's door and pulled out my phone. Fifi settled himself beside me. I called Marcus.

"Where are you?" he asked when I'd explained I thought someone had been in the house.

"I'm standing next to the truck with Owen, Hercules and Fifi. I'm fine. I don't think whoever it was is still inside."

"Did you see or hear anything?"

"No," I said. "I'm all right. I promise. Mike's truck is in his yard. If anything seems wonky I'll go over there."

"I'm on my way," he said. "Don't take any chances. Just stay safe."

I ended the call and looked up to see Mike Justason coming across the driveway. "Hey, Kathleen," he said. "Are my dog and your cat conspiring again?"

"It's more like they're my in-house security," I said.

His smile faded. "Is everything all right?"

I glanced over at the house. "I'm not really sure," I said slowly. "Marcus is on the way. I think someone may have been in my house."

Mike swore softly. "You want me to take a look?" he asked.

"I appreciate the offer," I said. "But I know Marcus would say it's a bad idea. Anyway, I'm pretty sure whoever it was is long gone."

"That's fair," he said. "Just the same, I'll keep you company until Marcus gets here."

It wasn't long before Marcus pulled into the driveway

behind my truck. He walked over to us. Fifi looked up at him and Marcus laid a hand on the dog's head for a moment. "You okay?" he said to me.

I nodded.

He turned to Mike. "Hey, Mike," he said. "You see anyone around the house today?"

Mike shook his head. "No. I've been here all afternoon, in and out of my house, and I didn't see or hear a thing. Fifi was outside pretty much all of that time and he didn't bark once and you know how he is about people he doesn't know."

Marcus nodded. "I'm going to take a look inside."

"How about I come with you?" Mike offered.

Marcus hesitated. "All right," he said. He looked at me. "Just stay here, please."

"Okay," I said. "You'll see the basement door is closed. I left it open just a little for Owen, the way I always do. And there was dirt on the mat. The mat I shook before I left."

He gave my arm a squeeze and the two of them disappeared into the backyard. Both cats kept their eyes on the house. Fifi stayed close beside me. My initial anxiety was being replaced by anger.

Someone had been in my house.

My home.

My hands clenched into fists seemingly of their own volition.

Marcus and Mike were only in the house a few minutes but it felt longer. They walked back over to me. "There's no one inside," Marcus said. "We checked everywhere." He turned to Mike. "Thanks for your help. I appreciate it."

"Hey, no problem," Mike said. He looked at me. "If you need anything, anytime, you know where I am."

"I do, thank you," I said. I leaned down and took Fifi's furry face in my hands. "You are a very good dog," I told him.

"C'mon," Mike said, patting his leg. The dog went with him but he looked back at me twice and somehow that made me feel better.

"I saw the basement door and the dirt," Marcus said. "Come take another look and see if you notice anything else."

I frowned at him. "You believe me, right?"

"Of course I believe you," he said. "I want to see if we noticed the same things that seemed off."

We headed for the back door trailed by Hercules and Owen. "How did the person get in?" I asked.

"I think they picked the lock." We stopped at the bottom of the back stairs. "What was the first thing you noticed?" Marcus asked.

"Well, first of all, Hercules and Fifi were acting . . . odd," I said.

"What do you mean, odd?"

I pointed at the stoop. "They were sitting here, side by side. They kept looking at the door, and when I tried to take Fifi home he wouldn't budge. That dog is heavy and I couldn't get him off the step." I rubbed my left wrist with the other hand. "I know that doesn't sound like anything important but it's not the way either of them acts. And then when I stepped into the kitchen, Owen was waiting for me. He wasn't on one of the chairs. He hadn't left a decapitated frog in the middle of the floor. He wasn't in the basement plotting heaven knows what. He was waiting for me."

We went through the porch and stood just inside the kitchen door. "Tell me what you saw."

I pointed at the table. "See that chair?"

He nodded.

"It's crooked. I hate it when the chairs are crooked so I always straighten them before I leave. And they're too heavy for either cat to move."

"I noticed that," he said. "What else?"

"Like I said, the basement door was closed." I indicated the mat we were standing on. "And there's dirt on the mat."

"That's why people have a mat by the door, to catch the dirt."

"I know," I said. "But I shake that mat every morning. *Every single morning.* C'mon, you've seen me do it. And don't say Hercules probably tracked it in because one, you know how he is about getting anything on his feet, and two, there are bits of crushed gravel on that mat. There's no crushed gravel in my yard or Rebecca and Everett's."

I stepped to one side and Marcus crouched down to look at the bits of dirt on the small piece of carpet. When he stood up he raked his hand back through his hair. "Is there anything else?" he asked.

I hesitated for a moment.

"What is it?" he said.

"Wood smoke."

Marcus frowned. "What do you mean by wood smoke?"

"I can't smell it now but when I came in before I could smell wood smoke, very faintly. You know how when someone who smokes has been in a room for a while and when they leave it smells faintly of cigarettes?"

"I know."

"Well, it was the same thing here, only it was wood smoke I smelled, not cigarette smoke. There's no one anywhere around here who has a wood stove, and besides, I couldn't smell anything outside."

"I didn't see anything missing but you should take a look around," Marcus said.

I walked from room to room but everything was where it should be. Nothing had been taken that I could see. I stood in the middle of the living room and looked around. "Wait a minute, the painting," I said. I pointed at the small canvas with one sunflower in a small glass bottle painted on it.

"What's wrong with it?" Marcus asked.

I pointed. "It's crooked." The right corner of the frame was up just a bit too high. I stepped closer. "Look by the bottom right corner. There's a tiny scrape on the wall."

He leaned in for a closer look.

"Someone was looking at that picture," I said. "Or maybe even took it off the wall. It's one of the paintings I bought from the library yard sale. Remember I told you I thought they came from Rebecca, but Susan corrected me. Do you think any of the three paintings could have somehow belonged to Robert Hamilton?"

Marcus was still studying the tiny scrape on the wall. "Robert Hamilton isn't missing any other pieces of artwork."

"That he's admitting to," I said. "We should check on the other painting."

Marcus straightened up. "Where is it?"

"It's in the storage space in the spare room."

We went upstairs to take a look and the painting was where I had left it, in a box in the small storage space under the eaves. There was no sign that anyone had been in the room and unless someone knew the layout of the old farmhouse they never would have thought to look there in the first place.

We went back down to the kitchen. Owen was standing by the refrigerator next to his dishes. He looked at his water bowl and meowed loudly.

"I'll just get him a drink," I said. I leaned down to pick up the bowl and stopped. "There's blood here on the floor."

Owen meowed again.

"Is he hurt?" Marcus asked.

I leaned down and picked Owen up. I checked him over carefully while he squirmed and grumbled. He wasn't hurt but I did find a tiny bit of blood on one of his claws. "I think he might have clawed whoever broke in," I said. I held up the paw so Marcus could see for himself.

"I should get someone over here to swab that blood," he said.

I set Owen down on the floor again. He gave me an indignant look, shook himself and, no surprise, disappeared. I pointed to the spot where the cat had just been. "How are you going to get a sample of that tiny bit of blood on his paw? You think Owen will cooperate?"

Marcus rubbed the space between his eyebrows. "I don't know, but we can still get a sample of that smear of blood on the floor." He took out his phone and moved a couple of steps away from me.

The crime scene tech who showed up was a young woman named Janice whom I had seen a couple of time before at Marcus's crime scenes. She was about average height with light brown hair cropped very close to her head and a serious expression.

Owen and Hercules sat in the living room doorway and watched her work. "Are they your cats?" she asked me, inclining her head in their direction.

I nodded. "The tuxedo is Hercules. Owen is the gray tabby."

I watched her take a sample of the gravel on the mat.

"Do they like people?" she asked.

I glanced over at the boys, who weren't paying the slightest amount of attention to me. "For the most part they do," I said. "But they were feral so they don't like to be touched."

"Most days I feel the same way," she said with an offhand

shrug. She took a sample of the blood by Owen's dish, then she looked up at me. "Detective Gordon said one of the cats has a bit of blood on a claw. You think I could swab it?"

"I can't make any promises but I'm willing to hold him if you want to try."

She got to her feet. "Let's give it a shot. Do you have any sort of treat the cat likes?"

I nodded. "Sardine crackers." I got three from the cupboard, set one in front of Hercules and held on to the other two as I picked up Owen and walked over to stand in front of Janice. He eyed her with curiosity but made no move to try to get away, understandable since I was still holding on to the crackers.

I offered him one and he took it. I caught hold of his paw and held it up. He shot me a glare of annoyance. "By the second toe," I said to Janice.

"I see it," she said. She swabbed the blood, careful not to make contact with the cat in any other way. "Thank you, Owen," she said once she was finished.

"Mrr," he replied around a mouthful of sardine cracker. I put him down and set the other cracker on the floor in front of him.

"That went okay," Janice said to me.

Considering that Owen could have clawed her, bitten her or just become invisible, I thought it went more than okay.

Janice continued to collect evidence with two furry supervisors eyeing her every move. Marcus's phone rang just as she was leaving.

He ran a hand twice through his hair before the very short phone call was over. When it ended he turned to me. "I'm sorry, but I have to leave. Please go stay with Maggie or Roma. I don't know if this break-in is related to Will's death but whether or not it is, it would be better if you were somewhere else until the locks are changed."

"I'll go out to your house," I said. Hercules and Owen had been there once and had had a grand time exploring. I didn't like being forced out of my own home and I wasn't going anywhere without the boys. I knew both Roma and Maggie would say bring them along if they knew about the break-in but I could foresee all sorts of problems.

"I'd like it better if you were with other people for now," Marcus said. "I won't be that long, an hour maximum. I'll call you and pick you up wherever you are."

"What am I going to do with the furballs?"

"It's pretty clear they can defend themselves." He glanced at the door. "I really have to go. I'll call you soon."

Marcus was gone before I had a chance to say anything else. I locked both doors and set a chair in front of the one in the porch. I had no illusions that it would deter anyone trying to get in, but they wouldn't be able to sneak in quietly. Maybe it was naive on my part but I didn't think whoever had been in my house would be back while I was home. They'd made a point of breaking in while I was at the library. Why come back when I was here?

I called Maggie but all I got was her voice mail. I tried Roma next. The same thing happened. I knew I could just show up at either one of their front doors or wait outside if they weren't home until they were, but I didn't want to do that.

I picked up my messenger bag and set it on the table. Hercules came right over to me.

"Merow," he said.

"How about we have a sandwich and look up a couple of things?" I said. "Then we'll go over to Marcus's house." Maybe I should have been afraid to be in the house, but I wasn't. The doors were locked, it was light outside and I knew Mike was home next door.

I made a turkey sandwich and got out my laptop. I didn't think the sunflower painting was valuable. The quality of the work was that of a very good amateur. Ruby had seen the painting a couple of times and I felt she would have said something if she thought I had a valuable work of art hanging in my living room.

I didn't think the small painting that was in the box in the crawl space was valuable, either. Although it wasn't of a door or a window, I felt fairly certain it was Daniel Gunnerson's work. That left the third painting, a slightly abstract watercolor of boats in a fishing port that I insisted to Marcus was in Spain. I remembered thinking when I first noticed the painting that there was something special about it, about the way the artist had captured the scene. I didn't have that painting. It was at Marcus's house.

Hercules and I looked through screen after screen of images based on the description of the painting I'd typed into a search engine.

"This is a gigantic long shot," I said to the cat. One ear twitched but he didn't look away from the computer.

And then we found it, just when I was about ready to give up. Technically, I think Hercules found it first. It was the watercolor that I'd hung in Marcus's hallway two years ago. I knew that painting well. It didn't take long to find its provenance.

It was titled *Fishing Village*. It had been stolen from a gallery almost eight years ago. Was Reese Winters right about Robert Hamilton? Had he acquired that stolen painting and then two years later it in turn was stolen from him? But how was Will mixed up in all of this?

Or was he?

chapter 14

I leaned back in my chair and looked at my watch. It had been more than an hour since Marcus had left. I'd completely lost track of time. I felt a twinge of guilt because he'd assumed I'd leave right after he did and I hadn't. I picked up my phone and tried his number. He didn't answer. He'd said he'd be no more than an hour, but whatever he was doing must be taking longer. I decided I would drive over to his house and wait for him there. Hopefully I could convince him to bring Micah back here for the night.

"Want to go to Marcus's house?" I asked Hercules. He made a face, jumped down from my lap and headed for the porch, walking through the door as though it wasn't even there.

I called for Owen. No response. I went down to the basement and up to my bedroom but I couldn't see him in either spot. I knew that didn't mean he wasn't there. It just meant he didn't want me to know if he was. I was going to have to leave Owen behind. I knew I could spend hours looking for him and he wasn't going to show himself until he was good and ready.

I rechecked all the windows and the front door to make sure everything was locked. I grabbed my purse and my jacket and went out into the porch. Hercules wasn't there. He must have gone out into the backyard. I locked up and went to look for him. There was no sign of the little tuxedo cat. I was going to have to leave him behind, too. I reminded myself that he could get out of pretty much any situation and Owen could disappear anytime he wanted to. They would be safe.

I drove out to Marcus's house but his car wasn't there. I tried his phone again and got his voice mail again. I wanted to go look inside the house and see if the painting was in its usual spot but I knew that was a foolhardy thing to do. If someone had been in my house they could have been in his as well.

"It's like one of those old movies where the heroine goes down into the basement during the power failure with the serial killer on the loose and a blizzard raging outside," I said out loud. I always made fun of those movies.

There was a meow of agreement from the empty space next to me, or what looked like an empty space, and after a moment Owen winked into view.

I shook my head. "You're getting way too good at this."

He sat up straighter as though he was pleased at my words. "That's not a compliment," I said sternly. My phone rang. "That's Marcus."

But it wasn't him. It was Riley. She was speaking so softly I could barely hear her. "Marcus is here," she said. "You have to come. He's messing everything up."

"Where are you?" I asked.

"At the farm."

So much for staying away from her grandfather.

"And Marcus just showed up. They're arguing about Duncan. He's making everything worse."

I assumed she meant Marcus and I wasn't sure he would listen to me. He'd gotten very close to Duncan and I wouldn't be surprised to find he had gone to confront Gerald Hollister over something involving the child. "Why are *you* at your grandfather's house?" I said.

"I don't have time to explain it," Riley said. "Just come, but use the back way. Remember I told you about the gate? I'll find you."

The call ended abruptly. I glanced down at my phone. The battery was dead. I normally plugged it in to charge as soon as I got home but because of the break-in I hadn't. I looked over at Marcus's house. I could let myself in and use his phone to see if Eddie was home. Eddie was a lot closer to the Hollister property. Maybe he could go over and get Marcus to leave.

Then I remembered the gate. I'd have to explain how to get onto Hollister land via the back way. It would take too long.

Plus Riley knew Eddie, but would she trust him in this circumstance? And would she trust me if Eddie showed up instead of me? I had told her to call if she needed me and now she had. I realized the best thing was to just go out to the Hollister property and see what was going on for myself.

I started the truck and headed up the hill. "Why did Marcus go out there by himself to talk to Gerald?" I said, to myself as much as to Owen.

"Merow," Owen said.

I sighed. "It had to be personal. Marcus wouldn't have gone out there alone on police business."

I knew how much Gerald didn't want Riley and Duncan living with someone else or even spending a lot of time with other people outside of his circle. That included me. Gerald didn't like me. He believed I had called Child Protective Services on him and Lonnie. I hadn't—Rebecca had—but I would have if she hadn't beaten me to it.

And Gerald didn't like anyone involved in law enforcement. I wondered why he suddenly cared about Riley and Duncan, because he never really seemed to bother with them before Lonnie went into rehab and they went to live with Lita. "Pride, maybe," I said to Owen.

The cat made a noise that sounded like skepticism.

"Could there be money connected to the kids somehow? Maybe Bella left something like a life insurance policy when she died."

"Mrr," he said. He seemed to think that idea had promise.

I remembered what Rebecca had said about Gerald. "Gerald is like a raccoon, except instead of collecting shiny things he collects things about people's lives that he can try to use for his own benefit." My chest felt as though I were being squeezed by a giant hand. In my mind I replayed what Reese Winters had said about her mother's affair. The man's name was Wyatt Hagen.

"He owned the landscaping company that was working at the house," Reese had said. "Mom always believed someone who worked for Wyatt had told Robert about the two of them."

And what had Rebecca told me? Gerald had once worked as a bricklayer for a landscaper.

"It was Gerald," I said.

I glanced at Owen. He looked confused.

"It was Gerald. It had to be. At one point he worked for a landscaping company. What if he worked for the man who had the affair with Robert Hamilton's wife? Gerald has been at the edges of everything almost from the beginning." My mind was racing.

I knew the back way onto the Hollister property because I'd been there before. There was no traffic behind me so I drove slowly, watching for a post with peeling green paint. That was where I needed to turn off the main road. At one time there had been a piece of yellow flagging tape tied to a tree beside the post but that was long since gone.

In the end I missed the turnoff, spotting it too late. I made an illegal U-turn and went back, turning down the gravel road into the woods. The road ran behind Gerald's property and Wisteria Hill. I watched for the broken-down fence and sagging wire that marked the line between Hollister land and Roma and Eddie's property. I finally spotted it.

I pulled the car over as far as I could. "You can't come with me," I told Owen. "It's not a good idea. I need you to stay in the truck."

He blinked his golden eyes at me and disappeared.

"Owen, I mean it," I said to the space where I'd last seen him. I tried my best to get out of the truck without letting him slip out as well. I gave a slightly hysterical laugh thinking how I was trying to not let my invisible cat get out of the vehicle.

There was an old tarp in the back of the truck. I grabbed it and crossed the dirt road. The narrow shoulder dropped down steeply to a wide, muddy ditch. The fence began on the other side. There were bushes and spindly trees growing through and around it. The wire was barbed and the fence seemed lower than I remembered from the last time I'd been there almost three years ago.

I made my way down the bank and through the wet, overgrown ditch. Then I opened up the tarp and threw it onto the wire at the lowest point closest to me so I could make it over the fence without getting snagged by the barbs. The fence had sagged significantly and I was grateful that Gerald had always been lazy about maintaining his property.

I got pulled at and scraped by the bushes and spindly trees

but I got over the fence and didn't get caught on the wire. No tetanus, no lockjaw. Score one for the good guys.

It had been years since I'd been in these woods. I knew I had to head northwest and turned in what I hoped was that general direction. I wished I'd stopped to call Eddie. And that I'd charged my phone, although it didn't mean it would be working right now. Being down in a low area surrounded by big trees meant the signal could have been blocked.

I walked for a good ten minutes and felt I had to be getting close. Then I spotted a lean-to up ahead in a small clearing. A gravel road curved away from it off to the left. The lean-to looked more like a section of an old barn left after the other half had collapsed. Gerald or someone had kept the brush cut back around it.

I stayed out of the open, close to the trees, looking for Riley. Something hit my shoulder. An acorn. I looked around and Riley was a few feet behind me peering around a tree. She had a welt on her cheek.

chapter 15

Riley held up a hand to let me know to stay silent. Why? Was Gerald somewhere close by? I eased my way through the bushes and the scrub to get to her. I was very relieved to see she was okay.

I tipped her face to look at the angry gash on her cheek.

"Did Gerald do that?" I asked in an almost-whisper.

Riley shook her head. "Tree branch," she said softly. She held up her wrist. "He did do this."

Dark bruises were already forming around Riley's forearm in the pattern of Gerald's beefy hand. I could taste something sour at the back of my throat. Very gently I felt Riley's wrist. She winced.

"I don't think it's broken."

"It's not," Riley said. "I've had broken bones before and I know what they feel like."

"Are you hurt anywhere else?" I asked as I looked her over. She was muddy and there were dried leaves in her hair.

"I'm fine," she said.

I gestured at her wrist. "How did that happen?"

Anger flashed in her eyes. "The old man tried to get Duncan from school. I stopped him."

"Where is Duncan now?" I asked.

"With Lita. He's safe." She looked past me, scanning the area around the lean-to.

I swallowed a couple of times, struggling to get my emotions in check. The next time I saw Gerald Hollister I was going to hurt him.

"What are you doing out here?" I said. "You agreed you'd stay away from your grandfather and the house." I felt a twinge of guilt. I'd promised Marcus I'd stay away from Gerald and here I was.

"I had to come out," she said. "I've been following the old man. It's okay. He doesn't know."

I couldn't seem to swallow down the sour taste in the back of my throat. "I don't understand," I said. "Why were you following him?"

Riley gave me a look. "Because I knew he was up to something. He's sneaky. I've been following him for the last week."

I stared at her, incredulous. "How?"

She gave an offhand shrug. "My bike, mostly. A few times I got a ride from this guy. That's where today went a little off track."

"What do you mean 'off track'?"

She waved my words away. "He got handsy. He thought I owed him something for a few rides. I didn't. Anyway, I figured the old man would come here so I rode up on my bike. Then Marcus showed up." Riley rubbed her wrist with the other hand. "I think one of the parents ratted me out over Duncan."

"What they should have done was call nine-one-one."

Riley rolled her eyes at me. "Yeah, because that works so well. Anyway, Marcus and the old man got into it. Marcus said if he didn't stay away from Duncan he'd arrest him. *He* said he'd see his own grandson anytime he felt like it."

"You were listening."

"They didn't know I was there." Her tone turned defensive.

Riley was pretty good at sneaking around. I didn't doubt that neither Gerald nor Marcus realized she'd been eavesdropping on them.

"Anyway, Marcus noticed something on the counter." She shrugged. "It might have been an envelope. I don't know. Whatever it was, I think Marcus figured out that the old man is doing something for the rich guy."

I was lost. I needed to figure out what was going on and find Marcus now. "Slow down," I said. "Which rich guy?"

"The one who just gave you money."

"You mean Robert Hamilton?"

She nodded. "Yeah, Hamilton. That's the guy's name."

"What makes you think your grandfather is doing something for Mr. Hamilton?"

"Because, duh, he was out here and gave the old man money. Why else would he give him money? Did the guy buy lunch and not have enough to pay for it? Not likely." She threw both hands up in the air. "Anyway, we have to stop talking and do something. Right before you got here the old man hit Marcus with something."

"What?" I said. "You should have told me that first."

"I was trying to," Riley said. "He's not dead or anything. I've been watching while I waited for you. Just before you showed, *he* pulled Marcus into the tunnels. He's probably already gone. There's another way out."

"Did you call nine-one-one?"

She shook her head. "No signal."

I took a shaky breath and let it out slowly. "What tunnels are we talking about?"

"The ones that connect Hollister land to the land that used to belong to Ruby's grandfather."

"You mean underground tunnels?" I said.

"Uh, yeah. They wouldn't be tunnels if they weren't underground. They connect Blackthorne land to Hollister land. There's an entrance in the woods just behind that old barn, which isn't as falling-down as you might think." In his day Ruby's grandfather had been the town bootlegger.

"We need to get help," I said. I heard a rumble of thunder in the distance. "My phone is dead."

"Wouldn't matter," Riley said. She held up her own phone. "I told you. We can't get a signal. All the trees and the weather—rain and thunder—have messed up the signal."

"Show me how I get into those tunnels," I said.

Riley turned to the left and began working through the trees. I followed her.

"Tell me what it's like inside."

"There's not a lot of room," she said.

I felt a frisson of fear crawl up my back. I didn't do very well with small, closed-in spaces.

"My mother said the ground here is sandstone with limestone on top. Millions of years ago this was all a huge sea, which is just perfect for those layers of rock to form and then over time for caves and tunnels."

Okay, so solid walls, not something dug out of dirt. The thought didn't make me feel any better. But that didn't matter. Going into the tunnels was faster than walking back out to get a signal and call for help, and all I could think about was Marcus.

"What are we going to do?" Riley asked.

"*You're* going to show me the entrance to the tunnel and then hike out to the road and call for help as soon as you can get a signal. *I'm* going to get Marcus."

We made our way up behind the lean-to. Then Riley turned left into the denser growth of trees. The ground sloped uphill.

She pressed her finger to her lips and I nodded. I tried to make as little noise as possible, paying attention to each step I took. I really hoped Gerald was long gone, but we couldn't be too careful.

We walked for several minutes and then came out into a small clearing. Right in front of us was an outcropping of rock covered with grass and other vegetation. The ground under our feet was a layer of decaying leaves and pine needles.

The opening to the tunnel was maybe five feet high, no more. Looking at it, I suddenly felt unsteady on my feet. Even though I was standing out in the open, it seemed like I could feel those stone walls pressing against me.

I took several slow breaths. I pictured Marcus's face. There wasn't anything I wouldn't do for him so I'd do this.

"We have to duck to get inside but after a few feet the tunnel drops and we can stand up," Riley whispered.

I shook my head. "Me. Not we."

Riley started to object. I shook my head vehemently then I bent it close to hers. "I need you to go get help. Marcus could be hurt." I'd seen that stubborn look on her face before. I put my hands on her shoulders. "Tell me what it's like inside. C'mon. We can't waste any more time."

"Once you can stand up you need to go forward, and when the tunnel starts to turn to the left stick with it," she said. "It opens up into a cave. That has to be where he took Marcus because that's where he stores things."

"What things?"

"Mostly things he's holding for other people. Things he doesn't want anyone to find. Keep one hand on the wall. There are some small spaces the water has made that you can step into if you hear Gerald coming. It's dark and he won't see you."

I nodded and concentrated on breathing. I looked up at the darkening sky and remembered something my mother would say if she was going to be away: The same sky that's over you is over me. The sky was still overhead even while I was inside the tunnel. It was still there.

I gave Riley a hard, tight hug and whispered, "Go."

"Here, take this," she said. She pressed the tiniest flashlight I had ever seen into my hand, looked at me for a long moment and then headed back the way we'd just come.

I ducked down and stepped through the opening of the tunnel. The ground underfoot sloped down very quickly. And after several steps I was plunged into complete darkness.

chapter 16

I stopped. I was shaking. I felt as though I was suffocating. I couldn't do this. I pressed one hand against the wall of the tunnel and pictured Marcus's face. *I'm coming. The same sky that's over you is over me. I'm coming.*

I managed to get the tiny light Riley had given me turned on. I directed it at the ground because I didn't want to risk shining it ahead of me and Gerald seeing it if he was actually still around.

Another few steps and I was walking in water but at least I could stand upright. I could hear squeaks and other sounds around me in the darkness. I refused to think about what I might be sharing space with. My breathing was labored like I was walking uphill with a heavy pack on my back, and my body was shaking, but I kept going forward, following Riley's instructions to stay left. The water was already over my ankles. Where was it coming from?

I heard something behind me. I stopped to listen but the sound had stopped as well. I continued on for a few more steps and heard the sound again. I whipped around, thrust out my arms and grabbed . . . Riley?

I pulled both of us against the wall of the tunnel. "What are you doing here?" I whispered. "You were supposed to go for help."

"I'm here to help," she said. "You can't get Marcus out by yourself if he's hurt."

I didn't know whether to hug her or yell at her. I settled for hugging her. "I'm going to yell at you later," I said against her ear.

"I'll go first because I know the tunnel better," Riley whispered.

"Absolutely not," I hissed. I put her behind me. "If we see your grandfather I want you to turn around and get out of here, run until you can get a phone signal and get help."

I could barely make out her expression in the beam from the tiny flashlight but I felt certain she was staring up at the tunnel ceiling, not looking at me. "Riley, I mean it," I said. I rested my hand against her cheek for a moment. "I couldn't stand it if anything happened to you."

After a moment she gave a grudging nod.

We started forward again, the water slowly getting deeper as we gradually went downhill and the tunnel got narrower. I noticed a section that seemed to lead off to the right. It looked wider. Was that the other way out Riley had mentioned? In another two or three minutes we passed a spot where I saw water coming out of the walls. Then at last the tunnel widened.

Riley's arm shot forward and she pushed me into an alcove in the rock wall. I could feel water running behind me at my back. For a moment it felt as though the rock was pushing back against me. I thought about how when this was over I was going to punch Gerald right in the face.

Ahead of us the tunnel opened into a cave, a wide space a bit more than six feet high and probably twelve to fifteen feet wide. Marcus was slumped against one wall, water over his legs. His eyes were closed and I wasn't sure he was conscious. Gerald was standing over him in hip waders and a heavy flannel shirt. There were several large metal containers the size of small refrigerators at the far right end of the cave, which sloped up a little. They were above all the water and were probably watertight anyway.

Gerald kicked Marcus with a booted foot and I pressed a wet hand to my mouth. Marcus didn't move or make a sound. I made a silent vow that I would make Gerald pay for this.

Gerald was talking and I leaned forward trying to catch what he was saying. "—more annoying than that little turd, Will Redfern." Gerald's voice echoed around the cave. "I dealt with him and I can deal with you." Even with the distance between us I could see something I wanted to believe was a long cat scratch on the back of Gerald's hand. *Way to go, Owen,* I thought.

Gerald came toward us and I flattened myself against the tunnel wall. Something ran over my foot and I bit down hard on my tongue so I wouldn't scream.

Instead of heading down the tunnel past us Gerald took the section to our right. I put my hand on Riley's arm and counted to sixty using my fingers. Riley, who loved math, caught on quickly to what I was doing. After I was sure a minute had gone by and Gerald was far enough up the tunnel, I moved toward Marcus. Riley followed.

I knelt in the water next to him and checked his pulse. His heartbeat was strong and I had to swallow down the tears that came with my relief at that. But he was injured and the water was still rising. I could see the wound on the top of his head where Gerald had hit him.

"Where is all this water coming from?" I said to Riley, who had crouched down next to me.

"The old man must have gotten someone to go open the old sluice gate," she said.

"What sluice gate?" I asked.

"It controls the water in the brook. It's been there forever, up-water of here on the other side of Hollister land. If it is open there's going to be a lot more water coming down."

I nodded. "We need to get out of here now."

Marcus opened his eyes. "Kathleen?" he mumbled.

"I'm here," I said. I found his hand and gave it a squeeze.

"You're real," he said. "Gerald killed Will."

"We heard. We have to get out of here. Can you stand?"

He nodded and then winced.

It took both Riley and me to get him to his feet, but once he was upright he seemed a little more alert. We moved back into the tunnel. The water was above my waist. We couldn't wade back through it. It would take too long.

"We're going to have to swim," I said. "Kick off your shoes."

I put Marcus and Riley in front of me. I swam with long strokes, taking care to keep my head above water.

We were maybe halfway back down the tunnel when I noticed that Riley was struggling to keep moving forward. She wasn't a strong swimmer. Suddenly she went under the water.

Marcus had her before I could get to them. He pulled Riley up out of the water and held her against his side as she coughed and wheezed.

I put one hand on her back.

"It's okay," Marcus said. "I got her."

Riley continued to cough.

There was no way out other than to swim. Wading through the almost-shoulder-high water was just too slow and in Riley's case the water was almost over her head. I needed a way to help her make it back to the entrance. I pushed back the sleeve of my shirt and realized I had two elastics wrapped around my arm. I'd taken them off the mail. Suddenly I had an idea. Riley had been wearing a pair of what looked like nylon splash pants. I'd seen her wear them before when she used her bike.

"Do you have bike shorts under those pants you're wearing?" I asked.

She nodded and had another coughing jag.

"Can you get the pants off?"

"Why?" she managed to choke out.

"Just take them off and give them to me." I slid one elastic off my arm and worked it through the buttonhole at the neck of my shirt. My fingers were cold and stiff and it took three tries. I pulled the other end up under the tiny clip at the end of the flashlight Riley had given me. I crossed my fingers it would stay put. Now I had light and free hands.

Riley had gotten her pants off. She handed them to me. I held my arms over my head and squeezed out as much water as I could from the pants.

"What are you doing?" Marcus asked. He sounded tired. I needed to get us all out of this tunnel.

"I'm making a flotation device," I said. I tied off the bottom of each leg of Riley's pants. Luckily there was a drawstring at the waist. That would help. My legs ached from treading water but I tried to focus only on what I was doing. I grabbed the waistband of the splash pants, brought them up over my head and then swung them down so they slapped on the water.

Just as I'd hoped, the legs filled with air. I pulled the waist ties tightly together and fastened the opening with my other elastic. My hands were just too cold to tie the waist. But it worked. I showed Riley how to tuck the makeshift flotation device under her neck and we started swimming again. It wouldn't last for long but I didn't need it to.

I couldn't seem to stop my hands from shaking anymore. I was breathing so loudly I sounded like a two-pack-a-day smoker. My claustrophobia was getting the better of me in the narrow tunnel.

Riley looked back over her shoulder at me. "Hey . . . you okay?" she said.

All I could manage to do was nod.

"She's claustrophobic," Marcus said. His voice sounded weaker than it had before.

"I didn't . . . think you were afraid of . . . anything," Riley said.

The flashlight banged against my collarbone. I was actually grateful for the chilling water that made it hurt less.

"I'm afraid of . . . lots of things. 'You must do the thing you think you cannot do.' Eleanor Roosevelt."

"She doesn't sound like she was a lot of fun."

"She was . . . stubborn. You probably would have been friends."

"All three of you," Marcus said.

Riley made more progress when she was distracted, I realized.

"You still want to be . . . a vet?" I asked.

"Not sure," she said. "Did you always want to be . . . a librarian?"

"For a while I wanted to be a professional pinball player."

"Is . . . that a thing?"

"Don't know." It felt like the tunnel was squeezing in against me. Then I realized it was. We were getting close to the entrance. "We're almost there," I said.

Marcus suddenly slumped face-first into the water. Two long strokes and I was beside him. I put my feet down and pulled his head up out of the water. He was unconscious. The water was just at my waist.

"Help me roll him onto his back," I said to Riley. Between the two of us we managed to get Marcus on his back. He was breathing. His pulse was steady. His head injury plus all the exertion in the cold water had just caught up with him. At least that's what I told myself.

I hooked my arm across his chest under his armpits and began to move forward. Riley grabbed the neck of Marcus's shirt. Our progress was slow but we were moving and the water level was dropping.

"I loved books," I said.

Riley looked over at me. "What?" she said.

"I loved books. That's why I became a librarian."

"I want Duncan to go to college," Riley said. She coughed again.

My flashlight winked out. I gave it a shake and the light came back on. "That can happen," I said. "Gerald is going to jail so you don't have to worry about him anymore."

"I want Duncan to have a family," she said in a low voice. "A real one who will keep him forever."

"That can happen, too," I said. "For both of you."

All at once I could see light up ahead. The tunnel rose up to meet it and the water level dropped dramatically. "We made it," I said to Riley. "We made it."

Somehow we managed to drag Marcus out of the opening to the tunnel. Like so many teenagers, Riley seemed to have a store of resilience. I dropped to my knees next to Marcus. I checked his pulse again. It was still steady.

Riley was patting her pockets.

"What's wrong?" I asked.

"I lost my phone," she said. She turned toward the entrance to the tunnel. "I recorded everything the old man said."

I shook my head. "No. We don't need it. My word and yours and his—I put a hand on Marcus's chest—will be enough." I reached for Riley, who twisted away from me.

"No it won't," she said, and she was gone, back through the tunnel opening.

chapter 17

I dropped to my knees. My legs ached. I was wet and exhausted, but I was not losing Riley. I pulled Marcus back from the entrance to the tunnel, propping him against the trunk of a nearby maple tree. I didn't want to leave him, but I couldn't leave Riley in there alone, either.

I wiped away tears with a shaking hand and covered Marcus with my discarded hoodie. I bent down to kiss him. "I love you," I whispered. "I'm coming back."

I stuck my head through the opening to the tunnel and called for Riley. I didn't get an answer. I took a deep breath, let it out and stepped inside. I waded through the water until it was over my waist and then started to swim.

The little flashlight was still attached to my shirt and, even more surprising, it still worked. I paddled with one hand and held up the light with the other. It was very awkward going but I kept moving forward in the deep water. Everything hurt and I was more tired than I had ever been in my life. My legs seemed to get heavier each time I kicked.

Finally I caught a glimpse of an arm. My stomach rolled over. Riley was floating face-down in the water ahead of me.

"No, no, no, no, no," I said. I grabbed the edge of her shirt and pulled her back to me. My legs cramped as I treaded water, but I managed to flip her onto her back and hook my arm around her chest the same way I'd done with Marcus. I swam with one arm and cramping, aching legs, and finally I saw light ahead of us.

I pulled Riley out of the tunnel, laid her on the ground and dropped down beside her. She wasn't breathing. I looked up at the darkening sky, then I started rescue breathing as tears rolled down my face.

And then Riley coughed.

I turned her on her side. She coughed and choked but she was breathing.

She was breathing.

I draped my body over hers, whispering, "I got you," over and over again. Finally I managed to half drag, half walk Riley over to Marcus. I fell a couple of times but in the end we made it. I leaned her against the tree next to Marcus. "Stay there," I said.

She tried to get up. She was still coughing. I pushed her back down again. "Stay there," I repeated. I checked Marcus. He was still unconscious.

We needed help. I made my way over to the tree where I'd stashed my phone in the crook of two branches. Was there any chance there was service and enough battery to call for help?

The phone was gone.

I felt the hairs rise on the back of my neck, the same sensation I'd had at Duncan's ball game when Gerald had been watching me. Slowly I turned around and across the open space I saw him standing holding my phone. He looked at me, then dropped the phone on the ground and stomped on it with one booted foot.

I was breathing hard and ragged. My legs were wobbling. Gerald gave me a triumphant look and I was suddenly seized with a burning fury.

Without really thinking I picked up a rock. It was heavy and rounded, about the size of a softball. Gerald smirked and began to walk toward me.

I didn't think. I just acted. I took two steps forward. I pictured Duncan instructing me on how to throw a ball. I held the rock the way he had showed me to hold the ball—like a set of fangs with my middle and index fingers. I turned so my left shoulder was pointing where I wanted the rock to go. In my mind I saw it hitting the side of Gerald's head. I threw with every last bit of strength my shaking arm had.

The rock glanced off Gerald's shoulder. He shook his head,

gave a snort of laughter and kept on coming. I grabbed another rock and ran at him, throwing with more fury than finesse, but somehow it was enough. This rock hit Gerald square on the right temple and he crumpled to the ground.

Somehow I managed to stay upright. I staggered over to Gerald and kicked the sole of his left boot. He didn't move. I pulled the laces out of my shoes, sat on his back and tied his hands together. I had nothing to tie his feet with. I looked around and spotted a huge broken tree branch. I grabbed one end and began to drag it toward Gerald. Halfway there it suddenly got easier. Riley had grabbed the other side. She was a bit unsteady on her feet but the two of us managed to drape the branch and another equally large one on top of Gerald. I don't know where we got the energy. Maybe it was the same kind of strength people get when they lift cars off of someone. Once I felt certain Gerald couldn't easily get up I checked his pockets. He had no phone.

I put an arm around Riley and together we made our way back to Marcus. I dropped down beside him. He was still breathing just fine and I thought his color looked better. I turned to Riley. "Are you all right?" I asked.

She nodded. "You came and got me," she said, "even though you're afraid of small spaces." She sounded . . . surprised.

I put my arms around her. "I will always come when you need me," I said. I decided I would rest for a few minutes and then I'd walk out to the truck.

Then behind us I heard something that almost sounded like a cat meowing in the near darkness. I looked up and, incredibly, Owen was coming toward us, stopping every few steps to shake his feet. He was very wet and, from his expression, very annoyed, and he was carrying something in his mouth. As he got closer I realized it was an old flip phone. He dropped it onto my lap.

"That's the old man's phone," Riley said. She looked at Owen. "How did he get that and how did he get here?"

"I don't know how he got the phone. I'll explain how he got here later." I picked up the phone and to my surprise it had a signal. I would have cried with relief but I didn't have the energy.

I kissed the top of Owen's head. "You saved us," I said.

"Mrrr," he said. Then he climbed up on Riley's lap and leaned his head against her chest. She looked at me wide-eyed and tentatively began to stroke his fur. Owen started to purr.

After everything else that had happened, why not this? I dialed 911.

Once I knew help was on the way I pulled Marcus against my side and put my arm around him. "I love you," I said. "Help is coming."

I put my other arm around Riley. Owen was still on her lap. I kissed the top of Riley's head. "And I love you," I said.

After a moment Riley whispered, "I love you, too."

chapter 18

It didn't seem that long before help arrived. I heard sirens and then Officer Stephen Keller's voice calling my name.

I waved an arm. "Over here." I eased Marcus against Riley's shoulder. "Watch him, please," I said. I got to my feet and stepped out into the small clearing, continuing to wave my arms.

Officer Keller came around a clump of trees and my whole body went weak with relief. I walked toward him realizing how I must have looked, wet and dirty and missing my shoes.

"Ms. Paulson, are you all right?" he asked.

I nodded. "I'm fine but Marcus needs help. He's been hit over the head. I think he has a concussion."

"Paramedics are right behind me," he said. "What happened?"

"He had some kind of encounter with Gerald Hollister." I pointed to where Gerald was stirring. "That's who hit him." Ric Holm and his current partner were making their way through the trees toward us with their gear.

"I'm going to take a look at Detective Gordon," Officer Keller said.

He walked toward Marcus and Riley.

"Hey, Kathleen, what's going on?" Ric asked.

I explained what had happened to both Marcus and Riley. "Marcus was conscious, but he passed out again."

Ric nodded. "What happened to your head?"

"Nothing," I said. "Just please look at both of them. Riley almost drowned."

He put a hand on my arm. "Kathleen, you're bleeding."

"I might have hit my head with a tree branch but it's nothing, I swear."

Ric looked at his partner and gave his head a little shake. "Let's go," he said to me.

We walked across the clearing and discovered that Marcus was conscious again. Ric crouched down next to him. Officer Keller got to his feet and took a few steps away from us to call for more help, I guessed. Ric glanced at me. "Kathleen, let April take a look at your head."

I looked at the young woman. "Please check Riley first," I said, keeping my voice low.

She smiled. "Mama Bear. I get it." She knelt by Riley. "I'm April," she said. She handed her a towel and Riley used it to dry off the cat, who was still on her lap, instead of herself.

"Kathleen, is that Owen?" Ric asked as he checked Marcus's pupils.

"Yes," I said.

"Okay. So Riley is . . . special?"

"She absolutely is," I said.

"Don't touch the cat, April," Ric said. "Trust me. Not a good idea."

April looked a little uncertainly at Owen. "Why?" she asked.

"His social skills are lousy," Riley said.

Owen meowed loudly in agreement.

I gestured at Ric. "Riley, this is Ric. He's one of the good guys."

Ric kept working on Marcus but he told Riley where to find the little baggie of dog and cat crackers he kept in his kit and she happily fed some to Owen.

"What happened here?" Ric asked, tipping his head slightly toward Marcus.

I told him how Gerald tried to kill Marcus by leaving him in the cave and how he had confessed to killing Will Redfern at the library. Riley pulled out her wet phone—I hadn't realized she'd found it in the tunnel—and explained how she had recorded her grandfather admitting what he'd done to Will and, as she put it, "Some other stuff."

"Maybe someone can dry out the phone and retrieve everything," she said.

Marcus reached out one arm. "Kathleen," he said.

I took hold of his hand. "I'm here."

"Is Riley safe?" he asked.

I gave his hand a squeeze. "She's all right."

Riley, still holding Owen on her lap, leaned over into his line of sight. "I'm fine," she said.

He smiled. "Good." He looked at me. "Is Riley holding a raccoon?"

Everyone laughed.

"No," I said. "She's holding Owen."

"Owen?" He shook his head and winced.

"He needs to go to the hospital," Ric said. "He needs an X-ray." He moved a finger between Riley and me. "You two need to go as well."

"I'm fine," Riley and I said at the same time.

Ric smiled. "Don't start with me. No argument. You're both going."

April was cleaning the cut on my forehead. "This one needs stitches and that one"—she indicated Riley—"probably will need antibiotics given that she swallowed a fair amount of very questionable water."

After some back-and-forth debate it was decided that Marcus would go to the hospital in the ambulance that was already here. Ric had called for a second ambulance for Gerald Hollister. It was possible he had a concussion as well. Officer Keller would take Riley and me to the hospital.

"I can't go to the hospital," I said. "What am I going to do with Owen?"

"The cat can come with us," Keller said. "He can stay in my cruiser."

There was no way that would work. "Look, the fact that he's being all cute right now notwithstanding, that cat is not a people person."

"I know that," he said. He turned to Ric. "Okay if I take some of those animal cracker things?"

"Take the bag," Ric said.

No amount of treats was going to turn this into a good idea.

"What happens if you get another call?" I said.

He smiled. "Then I guess I'll have a new partner."

Owen meowed loudly in seeming agreement.

We pulled in front of the ER at the same time as the ambulances. Ric disappeared with Marcus. Gerald, who was in handcuffs, was also taken away to be looked at. April stayed with Riley and me as we were settled in an exam room.

Marcus had a concussion but the doctor said he'd be all right. They wanted to keep him overnight but he was balking.

"I'll talk to him," I told the doctor. A nurse took me to the room where he was being treated. She'd found scrub pants, sweatshirts and rubber shower shoes for Riley and me. Just being out of those wet clothes made me feel so much better.

Marcus was sitting up in bed. He smiled at me. "We're getting out of here soon," he said.

"No, 'we' are not," I said. I felt the press of tears and had to stop and take a breath. "I came closer than I ever want to get to losing you. Please, just do what the doctor says, stay here. For me."

He nodded and swallowed a couple of times before he spoke. "All right. But I have a question. Did you throw a baseball at Gerald Hollister or was I hallucinating?"

I leaned over and kissed him. "A little of both," I said.

I needed stitches for the cut on my forehead. Riley was fine. Her lungs were clear. They decided to hold off on the antibiotics.

"She's young and strong," the doctor—who didn't look old enough to be in medical school let alone out of it—said. "Keep an eye on her for the next few days in case she develops pneumonia."

"You're coming home with me," I told Riley. I needed to be able to watch her myself. "I mean, if you want to," I added.

She shrugged. "Yeah, I better because you shouldn't be by yourself."

I put my arms around her shoulders. "You took a lot of stupid chances, and if you hadn't Marcus might not be okay, but you can't ever do anything like that again. You understand?"

She nodded. "You saved my life."

"You saved Marcus," I said, "and helped catch Gerald, so we're more than even."

Officer Keller took us home. I realized we were getting special treatment because of Marcus and I decided this one time that was okay. Riley was still holding Owen, who seemed happy to be carried around by her forever. I called Lita to let her know what had been going on and then I called Rebecca to ask for some help.

Rebecca came with food and hugs and a calm, reassuring smile. She checked my stitches, remarking on how small, tidy and even they were. She wrapped her arms around Riley and told her how proud of her she was. And she smiled at Owen and told him she was proud of him as well. Then she made us toast with peanut butter and hot chocolate.

Owen waited more or less patiently outside the bathroom door while Riley took a long shower. She put on a pair of my pajamas and I settled her in the spare room. "If you need any-thing I'm right next door," I said. "Just call me."

"I'm fine," she said. I'd noticed she said that automatically, whether or not it was true. I looked at Owen, who was still settled on Riley's lap despite my no-cats-on-the-bed rule. "If Riley needs anything, come and get me," I told him.

"Mrrr," he said. Owen seemed to have made some connec-tion with Riley. Maybe he recognized a kindred soul. Maybe he was just being a cat. I had no idea what was going on, but given the kind of night it had been I decided I was just going to roll with things and not question them.

Marcus was released from the hospital in the morning. Riley came with me to pick him up. He looked so much better than he had the night before. He reached for me with one hand, pulling me against his chest and resting his chin on the top of my head. Then he stretched out his other arm to Riley. "I thought I was going to lose both of you last night," he said. "I don't ever want to feel like that again."

Riley, being Riley, couldn't let that go. "Well, back at you," she said. "Going to see the old man by yourself? Really dumb."

Marcus nodded. "You're right. It was. So how about just this once, do as I say, not as I do?"

"Or how about you just don't do that kind of stuff again?" she said.

I nodded. "Yeah, I like that idea."

He smiled. "I learned my lesson, believe me." He kissed my forehead just to one side of my stitches and Riley laid her head against my shoulder. If this was what a happy ending felt like I'd take it.

Gerald was charged with assault and attempted murder for what he did to Marcus and second-degree murder for Will's death. He immediately implicated Robert Hamilton in everything. When Riley's phone was dried out all the evidence against Gerald was still there. Whether or not what he'd done to Marcus had been on Robert Hamilton's orders, I wasn't sure.

My guess that Gerald had told Hamilton about his wife's affair was right. That had been the beginning of a loose relationship between the two, it turned out. When Hamilton needed something done that skirted the line between ethical and unethical, he called Gerald Hollister.

When Jameson Quilleran stole the six paintings, he also swiped another one—from Hamilton's very personal and not always legally obtained collection. Knowing that he'd be a suspect, Quilleran hid that painting and one other—the watercolor that Will had tried to steal—at the home of the woman he thought of as his grandmother. Before he could get back to retrieve them, she had donated them to the library yard sale, and because she was suffering from dementia she couldn't tell him what she'd done with the artwork.

When Quilleran told his new buddy, Will Redfern, about stealing the paintings when they were out drinking together, Will realized he'd seen the two that were missing—at the library. He didn't share that information with his new friend.

Will was arrested for assaulting me before he could grab either of the paintings. When he got out of prison, he came to the library to look around for them under the guise of making reparations to me. I could only guess how he'd felt to see one of them hanging out in the open. He contacted Jameson Quilleran pretending he'd just discovered the watercolor by chance. It was Quilleran who asked Anita for help with the alarm system. It was good timing on his part. At least part of the reason she agreed seemed to be because of her animosity toward Robert Hamilton. She had approached him for a donation to one of her causes more than once over the past several years. He had refused every time.

Will's mistake was trying to get money from Hamilton for the second watercolor—the one from Hamilton's private collection that was hanging in Marcus's house—before he even had the painting. Gerald Hollister's job had been to get the artwork and deal with Will. Gerald had been following Will. Marcus's best guess was that their altercation took place outside in the library parking lot or somewhere else close by. Will hit his head, probably on the edge of a curb after Gerald assaulted him, stabbing him with an awl. But he was able to get away and get inside the library, where he died.

Gerald had assumed that the second missing painting was in the building somewhere. It turned out he had come in several times when I wasn't working to look for it on the main floor. Levi had thwarted his attempt to get upstairs but because he didn't know about my dislike of Gerald, he hadn't mentioned it to me.

Then chance worked in Gerald's favor. He overheard Susan and me talking at the ball game and realized I might have the other painting at home. He was the one who had broken into my house.

The phone call Marcus had taken that night was about Ger-

ald trying to get Duncan from school. If Riley hadn't inter-
vened he might have succeeded. She'd been right about one of
the parents noticing. The father of one of the kids who played
baseball on Duncan's team thought there was something off
about the encounter. He couldn't get it out of his mind so finally he called Marcus, knowing he was a police officer.

"I know I shouldn't have gone out to confront Gerald,"
Marcus admitted. "I was just so angry I wasn't thinking
straight."

He'd been arguing with Gerald when he caught sight of an
envelope from a high-end, boutique hotel that Robert Hamilton owned on the counter behind Gerald.

"All of a sudden things started falling into place," he said.

Gerald had noticed when Marcus spotted the envelope and
hit him over the head before he had a chance to react.

"He'll spend the rest of his life in prison," Marcus said after
he'd finished filling me in on all the details. A very, very small
part of me pitied the man, but mostly what I felt was relief.

chapter 19

I went back to work on Thursday. Marcus was still off and restless. I came home to discover that he'd cleaned the upstairs carpet and washed all the windows inside and out. My stitches were itchy and he had a spectacular multicolored bruise under his hair on the side of his head, but otherwise we were all right.

Rebecca sent over beef stew for our supper, delivered by Everett. Like everything she made, it was delicious. "There's something I need to talk to you about," I said to Marcus after we'd both finished our second helpings.

"Okay, go ahead," he said.

I took a deep breath and let it out. "I . . . I want to see if Lonnie will agree to let Riley and Duncan live with us." I held up one hand so he wouldn't interrupt. "Lita loves the kids. And she's taken good care of them. But I also know she's been thinking long-term. She wants them to have a family situation that will last beyond them becoming adults. I think that's us. When I thought Riley might die in that tunnel I would have done anything, risked anything to save her and I realized how much I want to be there for her, how much I love her." It was hard to keep my emotions under control. I cleared my throat and swallowed a couple of times. "Will you consider it?"

Marcus smiled. "Yes. Absolutely."

"Thank you," I said. "Take as long as you need."

He was already shaking his head. "No, no, I mean I want to do it, not just think about it. I want those kids with us."

"You're serious?"

He was smiling again. "I've gotten really close to Duncan in the past couple of months. He's a great kid. And as for Riley, she's prickly and smart-mouthed and so damn frustrating sometimes, but I can't imagine her not being part of our life."

"Merow!" Owen said, winking into sight.

"And what gives with him and Riley?" Marcus asked.

I felt so happy I couldn't stop smiling. "I think Owen recognizes a kindred soul somehow," I said.

"Given everything I know about that cat, it's not surprising." Marcus reached across the table for my hand. "There's something I need to talk about, too." He gave my hand a squeeze. "After everything that's happened I realize that we should be living here after we get married. I know how much you love this place. I've decided to put my house on the market. Home is anywhere you are."

I looked at him and laughed. "Marcus Gordon, I love you," I said. "I would live with you in a tent by the Riverwalk with Riley and Duncan and all three cats and I promise you I would be happy. And we may have to do that because when Everett dropped off supper he told me he had an offer on this house and I told him to accept it so we could live in your house."

He started to laugh. "We're that Christmas story you like so much."

"'The Gift of the Magi.'"

He nodded. Then he stood up, pulled me to my feet and took my face in his hands. "Kathleen Paulson, it doesn't matter where our family is, as long as we're all together."

I kissed him and then laid my head on his chest. "Do you remember the day we met? You thought I was having an affair with Gregor Easton, who was my parents' age."

"The only thing I remember is thinking how beautiful you were and how I was sure I was going to say something stupid, and then when you started talking and you were smart as well, it just made me ten times more nervous."

"Why have you never told me this before?" I asked.

"Most guys don't want the woman they're in love with to

know what a total dork they really are. I just wanted you to see my suave, smooth side."

I tried not to laugh but didn't succeed. "Do you think we would have ended up here if it weren't for Maggie and Roma and what sometimes felt like half the town pushing us together?"

"Yes," he said at once. "Some things are up to chance and some things are meant to be. You and I are meant to be."

On Saturday Marcus and I went to see Lonnie Hollister. He looked better than I'd ever seen him. He'd lost weight and the bloated, dissipated look about him was gone. He looked us in the eye and spoke in a strong clear voice.

We asked if he'd be willing to let us become Riley and Duncan's legal guardians.

I'd already talked to Lita. I didn't want her to think anyone doubted her ability to raise the kids. "If it feels wrong to you, tell me," I'd told her. "Riley and Duncan are happy with you and I don't want to mess anything up."

"I'll miss them like crazy," she'd said, "but as I told you before, I want them to have a family now and twenty—thirty—years from now. They have a lot better chance of having that with you and Marcus."

I found myself holding my breath as I waited for Lonnie's answer.

"Yes," he said. "Both of you have been good for them."

"Thank you," I said. "I give you my word we'll take good care of them."

"I'd like to stay in their life in some way," Lonnie said, "although that's going to be hard with Riley."

"Give her time," Marcus said. "You've got lots of it."

"I can't stay sober and come back to Mayville Heights to live. And I need to stay sober to have even a snowball's chance in hell with Riley." Lonnie swiped a hand across his face. "Even with my old man going to prison I have to stay away. I can't be a decent father, either. Not the kind they deserve. But I can work on being a better person, and that's what I'm doing." He smiled at me. "Bella thought of you as her friend and she'd be happy with this."

I smiled back at him. For the first time I believed that Lonnie was putting his kids ahead of everything else.

The psychiatrist who had been working with Lonnie agreed that he was incapable of taking care of Riley and Duncan and staying sober and was happy to tell that to the court. That would make the process of becoming their guardians easier. It wasn't the same as adopting both of them, but we would be a family in the ways that mattered and I decided I was just going to have faith that everything would work out.

We drove out to Lita's to talk to Duncan and Riley, with Lonnie's blessing, before we started the process. In the end their opinions mattered the most. As I sat on Lita's sofa I realized I'd never been so nervous in my life, not even when I proposed to Marcus.

"Do you mean like a family?" Duncan asked after Marcus explained that we wanted them to come live with us once we were married.

"Yes," I said, "but your dad would still be your dad and you could still see him and do things with him."

"But we'd all live together in your house and my grandpa wouldn't be able to take us away?"

"Yes, we would all live together, and no, your grandfather wouldn't be able to take you away," I said.

A huge smile lit up Duncan's face. He flung himself into my arms. "I think you'll be a very good mom and any stuff you don't know just ask me and I'll tell you."

"Thank you," I said, blinking away the tears that were suddenly threatening to overwhelm me.

Duncan hugged Marcus next. "So will it kind of be like I have two dads?" he asked.

Marcus nodded. "It will."

"Cool," Duncan said. "Can I go tell Lita?"

"Go ahead," I said.

He gave me another hug and ran outside.

Riley hadn't said a word. She had stayed leaning against the wall, head down, picking at the cuticle of her left index finger with her right thumbnail.

"We're not a package deal," she said once Duncan was gone. "You don't have to take me. I just want the squirt to have a good life and a real family."

Before I could say anything, Marcus took her by the shoulders. "I want you to listen really carefully," he began, then he stopped and he smiled. "But if you don't, that's okay because you're going to be hearing this as long as I have breath. You're going to get sick of hearing this." He leaned over so she had to look at him. "We want you. You. And Duncan. Not because you're a package deal but because we love both of you. You're stubborn, Riley Hollister, and you don't listen and I'm pretty sure we're going to bang heads on a lot of things. I want to teach you to swim decently and, Lord help me, how to drive, and I want to be there for every good and not-so-good moment in your life."

He looked at me over his shoulder and smiled. Then he turned back to Riley. "And you have to be blind not to see how much Kathleen loves you."

He took his hands off her shoulders and held his arms out, letting her know what came next was up to her. I held my breath as Riley looked at him for what felt like forever. Then she took a step forward into his arms.

After a moment she looked up at him. "Are you going to buy me a car?"

Marcus grinned. "Absolutely not," he said. Then he kissed the top of her head.

I stood up, brushed away a few stray tears and wrapped my arms around both of them. All I could think was that I was sorry for anyone who wasn't me at that moment.

That night Rebecca showed up. "I brought your wedding present," she said, handing me an envelope with white and yellow ribbons tied around it. Everett had already pledged whatever help we needed as we worked through the legalities of becoming the kids' guardians, and I hadn't been expecting anything else.

"What is this?' I asked.

"Open it and see."

I looked at the paperwork inside the envelope and then stared at her. "You bought this house," I said, incredulous.

"It's your wedding gift." She couldn't seem to stop smiling. "From me. I think Everett is getting you a toaster."

I handed Marcus the envelope without taking my eyes off Rebecca. "We can't take this. You can't give someone a house as a gift."

"Nonsense," Rebecca said, waving one hand in the air. "You and Marcus are giving Riley and Duncan a family. Why can't I give you all a house?"

"Bringing Riley and Duncan to live with us is something I did for myself as much as anyone else," I said.

"The same is true for me and this house," she said. "I want to keep all of you here. I want to watch those beautiful children grow up." She glanced at Marcus and raised one eyebrow. "And any others you might have. I'm kind of hoping I could be a surrogate grandmother of sorts. Please, please, take the house."

Behind me all three cats meowed in unison in case I somehow didn't know what they wanted. I looked at Marcus. He smiled and shrugged. And I said, "Yes."

chapter 20

And then at last it was our wedding day. The sun shone, the sky was clear and blue overhead and even if it had been raining I wouldn't have cared because Marcus and I were finally getting married. I hugged all three cats before I left the house. If Riley had had her way they would have been coming with us.

Ella had made a dress for Riley to match the other bridesmaid dresses. At first Riley had insisted she didn't want to be in the wedding, but when I told her how much it would mean to me she relented.

Duncan was a groomsman. Marcus and his father had taken Duncan to buy a suit. It was a "guy thing," Duncan had told me with great seriousness. The kids would be moving in in less than a month. Harry and Oren and Marcus *and* pretty much everyone we knew were working on an addition to the house. Hercules seemed to have appointed himself site supervisor.

Marcus and I spent as much time as possible with Riley and Duncan. Slowly, sometimes so slowly the change seemed infinitesimal, Riley was starting to trust us and this new life. She'd been to see Lonnie twice and I was hopeful that at some point she might actually begin to trust him, even just a little, as well. She regularly pushed and argued but Marcus had an infinite amount of patience and I remembered my own emotional teen years well, which helped.

Sarah and Hannah pulled Riley into their circle when they arrived for the wedding and the three of them did old, new, borrowed and blue. Riley's gift was borrowed and blue. It was a silver bracelet with a tiny blue stone that had belonged to Bella. I was touched.

"I'll take good care of it. I promise," I said.

"Yeah, I know," she said.

Sarah's gift was new, a lacy garter that she gave me with a saucy wink. "I'll help you put it on," she said. "It's Marcus's job to get it off." She laughed when I blushed.

Hannah gifted me something old—an antique locket with photos of Riley and Duncan inside. I knew it would go perfectly with my dress.

My mother came to help me get dressed. She looked beautiful in a pale lavender, tea-length dress. She would have looked beautiful in a black garbage bag.

Rebecca had styled my hair in a low knot with a few soft tendrils around my face and settled the flower crown of purple violets and lavender in place. Roma had done my makeup. All that was left was to put on my dress.

Mom fastened all the tiny buttons at the back and when I turned around she put a hand to her chest and drew in a breath for a moment.

"Oh, Kathleen, you are so beautiful," she said. "You took my breath away the first time I held you and now you're doing it all over again." She touched my cheek with one hand and I noticed she was wearing the bracelet of green beads that Duncan had made for her. "Today I feel nothing but happiness, because I can see how happy you and Marcus are. You're going to learn as a parent how much joy your child's happiness brings."

"You're going to make me cry," I said.

She leaned in and brushed a kiss over my forehead. "Love you, Katydid," she said.

There was a knock at the door. Mom opened it to Maggie and Roma, who had Duncan with them. He was wearing a dark gray suit with a white shirt and green striped tie.

"Wow, you look like a princess," he said.

I smiled. "And you look very handsome. I'm so happy you're here. Could I have a hug?"

"Riley told me not to get you all smushed before the wedding."

"I don't care if I get smushed," I said, "but how about we try a careful, non-smushy hug?" I bent down and Duncan put his arms around my neck.

"I love you," he whispered.

"I love you, too," I said.

"Okay, kiddo, we have to go," Roma said. She smiled at me. "See you out there."

Maggie blew me a kiss and the three of them were gone.

Mom straightened the back of my dress then stepped away to look at me again. "That's it," she said. "I can't improve on perfection."

There was another knock at the door. "That's your father," Mom said. "Are you ready?"

I nodded. "I am so ready." I had no nerves at all, just a few excited butterflies fluttering in my chest. I was ready to marry Marcus. I was ready to make a life with Riley and Duncan.

Dad, like Duncan, was wearing a gray suit with a white shirt and striped tie. It's what all the men in the wedding party were wearing. He looked as handsome as ever. He put a hand over his heart. "You take my breath away, Kathleen," he said.

"You look wonderful yourself," I said.

He leaned in to give me a gentle hug. "I was going to ask if you're happy but I can see it all over your face that you are."

"I am," I said. "You know, the only thing better than having everything is recognizing that you do."

He smiled. "I wonder what incredibly perfect man said that."

I smiled back at him. "One who is also an incredibly perfect dad."

He laughed. "Well, thank you for forgetting all my mistakes, at least for today."

I reached for his hand and gave it a squeeze. "You've always been a great dad."

He looked down at his watch. Ethan, Sarah and I had bought it for him several years ago for Father's Day. "You were my learning curve, Kathleen. Everything I know about being a parent is because I practiced on you."

"I'll make sure to tell Ethan and Sarah they owe me," I teased.

His expression grew serious. "I already love being a grandfather of sorts to Duncan and Riley. Duncan is so curious, so full of questions. And Riley." He shook his head. "She's smart and stubborn and intensely responsible." He gave me a look. "Sound like anyone you know?"

I held up my thumb and index finger about half an inch apart. "Maybe a little," I said.

"She's going to be a challenge but she's also going to bring you an incredible amount of happiness, just the way you did for me."

"I love you," I said

He leaned over and brushed a kiss on my forehead. "Love you, too," he said.

Mom poked her head into the room. "It's curtain time," she said. "Are you ready?"

I nodded. Dad offered me his arm and we walked out to start the rest of my life.

Marcus and I were married with a few tears and a lot more smiles and laughter. And then Rebecca performed a variation of a Celtic handfasting ceremony and, symbolically at least, bound Marcus and me and Riley and Duncan as a family. We stood in front of her, in front of our family and friends, Marcus on one side and me on the other with Riley and Duncan between us.

"People often say, 'You don't choose your family,'" Rebecca began. "But sometimes you do. These people, this family, chose each other."

Riley and Duncan joined their hands, right to right and left to left. I laid both of my hands on top of theirs and Marcus did the same with his. Rebecca held a long braided cord that Riley had made with help from Maggie. One strand was a piece of fabric that came from a blanket that had belonged to Marcus when he was a baby. There was a similar strip from a blanket that had been mine. The third strand was from the blanket Bella had made for Riley before she was born. It had been Duncan's as well.

Rebecca looped the cord around our hands and tied it together. "The love that binds you is stronger than any rope. It will hold you up in the best of times and in the worst. No matter where you go it will always lead you back home again."

Then there was Eric's wonderful food and after that music and dancing from Johnny Rock and his band, with Larry Taylor playing bass and my brother, Ethan, sitting in on guitar and singing a couple of songs. Oren even played the keyboard with them for one song.

My dad made a toast and so did Marcus's father. Maggie reminded everyone how half the town had conspired to bring the two of us together. And Brady shared how we made everyone around us believe in happy endings. Marcus danced with Riley, and I danced with Duncan. Then at last I was back in Marcus's arms.

He glanced down at the gold wedding ring on his left hand then smiled at me. "I have to say I like being married," he said.

"It's only been three hours," I teased.

"But they've been three very good hours." He leaned down and kissed me. And I knew, like in all the very best stories, we were going to live happily ever after.

acknowledgments

A well-deserved thank-you goes to my editor, Jessica Wade, who encourages, cajoles and corrects with heart and humor. Thanks as well to my agent, Kim Lionetti, who is part cheerleader, part voice of reason. To everyone at Penguin Random House who has worked so hard on this and every other book in the Magical Cats Mysteries, thank you from the bottom of my heart. You all make me look good. And thank you to the friends who shared their wedding stories—several of which I will take to the grave, I swear!

Lastly, thank you to Patrick and Lauren, who are always my ride or die.